Other Titles by TW Brown

The DEAD Series:

DEAD: The Ugly Beginning
DEAD: Revelations
DEAD: Fortunes & Failures
DEAD: Winter
DEAD: Siege & Survival
DEAD: Confrontation
DEAD: Reborn
DEAD: Darkness Before Dawn
DEAD: Spring
DEAD: Reclamation
DEAD: Blood & Betrayal
DEAD: End

DEAD Special Edition

DEAD: Perspectives Story (Vols. 1 & 2)
DEAD: Vignettes (Vols. 1 & 2)
DEAD: The Geeks (Vols. 1 & 2)

DEAD: Snapshot— {Insert Town Here}

*DEAD: Snapshot—**Portland, Oregon***
*DEAD: Snapshot—**Leeds, England*** (August 2015)

Zomblog

Zomblog
Zomblog II
Zomblog: The Final Entry
Zomblog: Snoe
Zomblog: Snoe's War
Zomblog: Snoe's Journey

That Ghoul Ava

That Ghoul Ava: Her First Adventures
That Ghoul Ava & The Queen of the Zombies
*That Ghoul Ava Kick Some Faerie A***
Next, on a very special That Ghoul Ava
That Ghoul Ava…on the Lam!

You can find my titles on Audio as well.

Audible.com

That Ghoul Ava on a Roll!

(Be prepared for a few "sports–themed" adventures.)

TW Brown

authortwbrown.com

Portland, Oregon, USA

i

A moment with the author…

Here we are. A new *That Ghoul Ava*. As I put the final touches on this one, I am also working very close with an amazing artist, John Donald Carlucci on the transformation of the *That Ghoul Ava* series to a graphic novel. This is a big step, and one that I am very excited about. It will open Ava to a whole new audience. (Hopefully.)

I really don't have a lot to say as I present this newest adventure to you. I would like to thank Brandy McQuirter for some very cool Roller Derby gear. Also, she was kind enough to shoot me a list of names. I hope I did not do any injustice to the ladies who sport the names on their jerseys that I used in this story. Also, I apologize for any inaccuracies that I may have spun regarding Roller Derby as a sport and what happens on the track.

If you do a little looking, I bet you will find a local Roller Derby group in your area. I would suggest you going and taking a look. If you do, and get a chance to take a picture with some of the athletes, feel free to send me a copy. The first one to do so holding up a copy of this book might just get an *Ava* tee shirt as a "thank you" from me.

Some quick thanks to my wonderful Beta Readers: Kate Sellar, Todd and Amy Strockoz, Caroline Harmon (official president of the *That Ghoul Ava* fan club), Kary Lawrence, and Terri Deese. Your help and suggestions make this a better book. I also want to thank Pamela Lorence. She is the voice of the audio book version of this series and now that I dabble in the narration field, I REALLY appreciate her hard work. I continue to hope that the audio version takes off like my *DEAD* series so you can start getting paid closer to what you so richly deserve.

"Look at all the people here tonight!"
TW Brown
January 2016

Contents

1	Roller	1
2	So Emotional	15
3	Bark At The Moon	27
4	Flying High Again	41
5	Too Shy	53
6	Private Eyes	61
7	Come On, Eileen	75
8	I'm Still Standing	85
9	You Dropped A Bomb On Me	95
10	Harden My Heart	105
11	Is There Something I Should Know	117
12	Turn The Page	129
13	You Spin Me 'Round	137
14	Bastard	147
15	Two Out of Three Ain't Bad	159

1

Roller

"Is this Ava Birch?" the sultry voice purred through the phone.

"Umm...yeah?" It sort of came out like a question.

I simply was not used to my phone ringing. In fact, I was so out of the loop in this department that I still keep an actual physical phone mounted to the wall in my kitchen. I have a cell just like any other person (and Supernatural). The biggest difference between me and...say...you, would be the fact that mine can actually have its battery die, and until somebody tells me that I need to charge my phone so they can reach me, it can sit in my purse and be just as dead as I am.

"I understand you...well, gads, I don't know how to put this." The woman was beginning to sound like she wanted to crawl under a rock. Holy cow, just spit it out already! That was what I was about to say before she continued in a rush. "I have a friend who tells me you specialize in things that...normal people might not necessarily deal with."

Now I was curious. However, she also sounded very much like a regular person. By that, I mean she sounded human...mortal...not Supernatural. If she was a human, then there might be a problem; the first would be how in the hell she got my number; a close second would be finding out who thought it was a good idea for her to call me.

"Listen…" I let that hang so that whoever this was would perhaps be so kind as to give me her name.

"Oh, sorry!" the woman purred.

Jeez, I was really not liking her already. Even sounding embarrassed came across as sexy in this woman's voice that reminded me a lot of Kathleen Turner from her glory days.

"Brandy…Brandy McKeon."

"Okay, Brandy, I am going to ask a silly question." I paused for dramatic effect, and then I asked, "What are you…exactly?"

"What am I?" She sounded confused. "Umm…well…I am a mom. I work as a nurse. But I am calling you because I am also a member of a roller derby team, the *Hot-n-Steamy Rollers*."

I hung up the phone.

Seconds later, it rang again and I did what most people do when their phone rings; I ignored it. I peeked out of my kitchen to see if anybody might be padding about at this ungodly hour of four in the morning and was happy to discover that I had the house to myself. Well, in a manner of speaking.

At last count, between the woods out back, the barn, the stables, and the house itself, there were currently one hundred and fifteen residents living (or some semblance thereof) on my property. I had been forced to sell my state-of-the-art house in luxurious Lake Oswego and now lived on an old Christmas tree farm in Estacada. Not that this house wasn't charming in its own right, but it was built about seventy or eighty years ago and lacked most of the modern amenities that I'd quickly become used to in my Lake Oswego home.

Adding to my dour mood, the last several days had been more than a little difficult for me and some of my housemates. We'd just lost some of our friends and loved ones in that last little encounter with a lamia. The one hit the hardest was the goblin, Nose Wart. He lost his mate in the battle to put down that particularly nasty monster. If I never see another lamia again, it will be too soon.

I'd had a few jobs up to this point, but nothing as gut-wrenching as that whole deal with the lamia. The fact that the creature ate children was only one part of the whole terrible ordeal. She'd poisoned Lisa and turned her into a nasty little bitch for a while. Also, she'd done a number on me each time we'd gone head-to-head.

Yet, no matter what any of us had suffered in that fight, it really did not compare to the loss experienced by the leader of my very own goblin clan. Nose Wart had lost his mate in the debacle and that was only made worse by the fact that I'd had to devour her corpse to stem my own injuries. One of the factors that goblins use when determining if they will choose another goblin as a mate is a taste test. Apparently the final act in any goblin marriage (or whatever they call it) is for the surviving mate to eat the deceased. Nose Wart had been denied that rite so that I could recover and continue to battle the horrific lamia.

I wondered sort of absently where my little goblin pal might be at the moment. *He is in the back yard, Ava,* a voice said inside my head.

That voice belonged to Nose Wart's former mate, Butt Pimple. As is apparently the case, I keep the soul or whatever from most of the Supernaturals that I consume in a space or something in my head. Don't ask me how it works. (Note from Ava: If this is the first of my adventures that you bothered to pick up, I'm gonna do my best to fill you in on stuff, but honestly, I am still learning all this crap for myself.)

I headed for the back door and paused when I reached it. With my hyper-sensitive hearing, I could detect some sort of sniffling. I did not need to be a genius to know that it was Nose Wart and that he was crying.

You must put an end to that nonsense, Ava, Butt Pimple growled in my head.

Jeez, give the poor guy a break. He just lost his wife and unborn goblin litter, I shot back.

He is the leader of our clan, he cannot be seen as weak or one of the others will challenge him for control.

Do I need to repeat the whole thing about losing his mate and unborn—

That does not matter to a goblin! Butt Pimple cut me off.

Interesting that she was almost antagonistic towards me now that she resided in my head with the others I had consumed which, to date, consisted of The Queen of the Zombies, an ancient creature called a gwyll, a boy who was versed in necromancy while likely not even knowing what that word meant, and a wizardy sort of character that, as far as I know, is still securely walled up in a dark corner of my mind.

I would get into this with her later, but for now, I wanted to see if there might be anything that I could do for Nose Wart. I did my best to wall up all the current residents of my head and stepped out onto the back porch.

The little goblin was sitting on the top step with his legs dangling over the edge. He had his head buried in his over-sized hands that were perhaps two or three sizes larger than something his size should sport. At first he did not appear to notice me, and I was about to speak when he made a disgusting snort that sounded like it sucked about a quart of phlegm back up his nostrils, followed by an equally repulsive gulping noise.

"Just Ava," Nose Wart sniffed as he scrambled to his feet and turned to face me. "Please forgive my weakness. If you deem it necessary to punish me, I shall accept your sentence."

"Umm…huh?" I sort of flopped down so that I was sitting beside the little creature and stared out into the dense woods of what had once been a Christmas tree farm.

I saw an occasional flit or flash of a faerie or their smaller cousins, the pixies. They loved having this little forest to themselves. And since I had promised to never allow it to be harvested, as well as my open invitation for them to do whatever it is that those sorts of creatures do in the woods, there was a lot of activity in those trees at night.

"My behavior is not fitting as a clan leader. I am an embarrassment to all goblins," Nose Wart exhaled as he continued to stand at my side.

I turned and stared into his beady little eyes and tried to remember my initial disgust at first encountering goblins. It seemed impossible that I could have ever felt that way now that I was coming to know these creatures. I'd come to see them more as puppies. Sure, they are still so damned ugly; but they are ugly in that cute way.

Nose Wart immediately averted his gaze so that he was not looking me in the eyes. Of course my first thought was that he was simply showing his subservience, and then I heard Butt Pimple snarl. *Stop being so weak, you son of an infected boar's testicle!*

How did you get out? I asked inwardly.

For whatever reason, Nose Wart could actually see his beloved in my eyes, sort of like he was looking through a window into my head where I "stored" these special Supernaturals that I consumed. I am sure it is more complicated than that, but I have been told (and not always in a complimentary way) that I have a knack for simplifying things.

I want you to demand that he cease this mourning, Butt Pimple snapped, ignoring my question.

And I want to remind you that I am the one calling the shots here, not you, little goblin, I shot back, mentally boxing her up and locking her away once more.

"She spoke to you," Nose Wart said. It wasn't a question. I had a feeling that I have been drastically underestimating the intelligence of goblins up to this point; that would have to change.

"She wants you to stop being so sad about her death," I replied, seeing no sense in telling him about how angry she gave the impression over his sorrow.

Nose Wart cocked his head and finally looked up at me. His large eyes were red and puffy from his crying. His lower lip quivered slightly for a moment and then he snapped his teeth together.

"I am Nose Wart, warlord and leader of the Goblin Vomit clan. This behavior will cease." I was not sure if he was stating it in general or if he was simply giving himself a personal bit of a reminder. He stood and went rigid, arms pressed to his side, legs as close together as a goblin with all that dangling junk could manage. It took me a second to realize he was standing at attention. "I am the servant and chief guardian of Just Ava, the ghoul warrior."

I was about to say something when I heard the jangling of my phone from inside. I decided that maybe now was as good a time as any to return to the kitchen and moseyed in to answer the phone. I guess I had already forgotten about the call from just a few minutes earlier; at least that was the case until I answered it and heard the woman at the other end.

"Valkyries," the female voice blurted in lieu of a greeting.

"Umm, what?"

"Our league has been infiltrated by a group of renegade Valkyries, they are hurting the girls…and yesterday, one of my team mates died in the hospital from her injuries," the woman said with a speed that would make an auctioneer jealous.

Okay, at least now I was listening. I shifted the phone to my other ear and grabbed the marker that hung by a little red string from our Dry Erase board. I scribbled the word "Valkyrie" and a large question mark.

"Before you say another word, I want to know how you got my information." That seemed like a logical way to get this started.

"My sister was the thrall of a vampire named Hector. Hector knows Belinda Yates."

Okay, I guess that could eventually lead to me. Of course I thought it more than a little strange that Belinda would be tossing my name around, much less recommending me for a job. She and I were nothing close to friendly with each other on the best of days.

"You do realize how that comes across," I said, trying my utmost to sound like a normal human might if they were told such things.

"Yes, but I have been dealing with your type—" Brandy stopped speaking so abruptly that I heard her teeth snap together. There was a brief pause where all I heard was her trying not to breathe. "I'm sorry, I didn't mean anything by that, I just meant…"

I let her squirm in uncomfortable silence for a moment after she trailed off. When I felt she had waited long enough, I finally spoke. "Listen, I don't know what you think you know about me, and I am not going to ask. How about you just tell me what it is that has prompted you to call me."

"It began about three weeks ago. The new season just started and everybody was really excited because there were two new squads set to join the league. We knew about one of the teams because the manager was a lady we have all skated with or against for years. The second team was a total mystery and nobody knew any of them. That is sort of strange because most of us know each other in some way or another. They called themselves The Valkyries and had roster names like Arifra, Arda Ovif, Hildegard, and Rodmadra, which most of us agreed was sort of peculiar."

"Why would that be strange? I mean, those are some funky names, but how about you tell me your reason for thinking that." I wasn't about to let on to the fact that I was probably more ignorant of roller derby stuff than I am about the Supernatural world. And if you have been along for these little adventures of mine, you realize the magnitude of my ignorance.

"You don't know much about roller derby, do you?" Brandy snorted, letting me know that my ruse was pretty much a bust when it came to me attempting to hide my total ignorance.

"No," I admitted. "Actually, until this phone call, I thought that roller derby had gone by the wayside back in the 80s."

"Our names have meaning. Some are plays on our personality, or they have a bit of a naughty double entendre."

"I don't follow."

"Well, for instance, my derby name is Meg Abbitch." It took me a second to actually hear it the way she intended. Naturally, I initially heard Mega-bitch, but then she spelled it out for me. "My...friend...the one who just died? Her name was Hal'Raiser." Once more she spelled it out to me for clarification. "And she was more than just a friend and fellow skater...she was my sister."

Now it was making a bit more sense as to why this woman was so invested in the problem. I only briefly wondered why she had not led with the whole thing being about her sister in the first place, but that was not really my top priority at the moment.

"Okay, let's get to the part about these women being Valkyries. I guess the first thing I want to know is how the hell you would come to such a conclusion." That seemed like a logical next question.

"Google." She declared that single word like it explained everything. After a few seconds, I pressed for more details. "I googled the names on a whim trying to figure out what sort of meaning they were trying to hint at and came up with Valkyries. I actually thought that I would discover that the words had some sort of meaning in a language like Norwegian or something."

"And these names they are using, all of them are the names of Valkyries?"

"It took some searching, but their manager and captain who goes by the name Gunnr was what helped the most. She is mentioned in some sort of famous poem about the Valkyries," Brandy answered.

"Okay, so you have a few possible Valkyries in your roller derby thingy," I offered, pinching the bridge of my nose as if that might stave off the headache that was trying to gain a foothold. I was a little surprised at that sensation. Ghouls can get headaches. Who knew? "What does that have to do with me? Why do I care?"

"Did you get the part about one of our ladies…my fucking sister! The whole part about her dying in the hospital from the horrible internal injuries she received at the elbows and shoulders of these bitches?" Brandy's sweet voice suddenly became hostile and angry. "They aren't human!"

The woman paused again. I could tell that she had more to say, but I was already sifting through what I knew. Big surprise! It wasn't much. In fact, I had to wonder about the whole "Valkyrie" thing and how it might pertain to the Supernatural community. I didn't know a lot, but I did know enough about Valkyries to know that they were warrior goddesses or something to that effect. I knew that they were Norse in origin. Did that mean that the mythological gods and goddesses were real? I pinched the bridge of my nose a little harder as my head began to throb.

"…and when my sister Haley died the other day, Hector showed up at my house." Crap, I was missing stuff. *Time to focus, Ava.* "It was me that had to explain what happened. He vanished before I finished speaking, but he came back about an hour later. He seemed…drunk, which is weird because I did not think vampires could get drunk. In any case, he showed up spewing something about Valkyries and kept saying that he needed to get ahold of Belinda since she apparently knew somebody that could deal with…and I am quoting him here, "whacked out Supernaturals who don't have the sense to follow the fucking rules." Then the sun came up and I had to shut him away in my basement."

"Wait, so he is at your place now?"

"Yeah, but it's okay, there are no windows in my basement, so he is safe."

That really wasn't my point. This woman was talking about having an actual vampire in her basement like she might be talking about a stray dog. I may not be all that tuned in to the whole Supernatural community, but I did know that I was speaking to a regular human who was blabbering on about vampires and Valkyries to a ghoul like we were just two girlfriends catching up on old times. She did not seem the least bit taken aback by any of this other than the part about how possible Valkyries killed her sister playing roller derby.

"So what exactly do you want me to do about this?" I finally asked when I realized that we had been in silence for several heartbeats.

"I want you to come down here and take those bitches out," she said with venomous anger. "I want you to make them hurt…make them pay."

All of a sudden, Brandy was not sounding anything like the sweet soccer mom. Her tone was cold and she meant every word she was saying. She was not using the word "kill" in a figurative manner; nope, she wanted me to *literally* kill them.

"Okay. First off, it does not quite work like that," I started.

"I already spoke to Belinda. Some woman named Morgan

called me ten minutes later and said that you could do the job," Brandy insisted.

Okay, that was interesting. I was about to say so when a knock came at my door. I already knew from the way the person knocking had simply touched the door a few times in such a way that it is likely I am the only person who heard that it would be Morgan, the regional Psychic, and sort of my employer.

"Tell ya what, Brandy…" I motioned for Nose Wart to go open the door as I unwound myself from my receiver phone cord that I always seemed to coil around body when I spoke on the phone. "How about you call me in ten minutes and I will give you my answer." I didn't wait for her to reply; I simply hung up and turned just as Morgan drifted into my kitchen.

"I take it you heard about the Valkyries," she said with no more emotion than if she was telling me about the weather.

"Yeah, what the hell is that all about?" I took a seat at my kitchen table.

"Looks like another trip to Texas for you." Morgan sat down and produced a small tea infuser with a smoky looking glass of amber liquid that she quickly uncapped and sipped from.

She might act like she was fine, but that beating that she had endured not too long ago was still taking its toll on her. Her normally lustrous hair had no shine to it and her smooth facial features looked like they might be threatening to reveal an honest-to-God wrinkle. If I really stared, I was almost certain that I could make out the slightest hint of crow's feet at the corners of her eyes.

She'd come to Texas while I was there dealing with a Psychic that wanted to take Morgan down and add me to his arsenal. Morgan had taken a beating at the hands of a freaking giant. I'd managed to transport her to the heart of a faerie Sidhe to allow her to receive some healing. Of course that had not sat well with the faeries. They had not liked the fact that my having devoured that gwyll named Blodwen gave me open access to their home. I'd made a vow in the heart of the Sidhe that I would not enter the faerie stronghold uninvited and also agreed to perform a task for Rain, the new Godmother. Are you starting to get the picture that my life can be a wee bit complicated?

As for Morgan, she was healed enough so that Betty was able to take over in regards to her general recovery. I still had a hard time accepting the fact that Morgan had vulnerabilities. After all, she's been around since the time of the honest-to-goodness Jesus if you believe her stories of her youth. Although none of that was as remarkable as the fact that she'd submitted to Betty for her recovery regimen.

I knew that Betty was dosing her with something on a regular basis, and from the smell of the tea, I would have to guess that this was more of her many herbal treatments.

"Why would you want me to go to Texas?" I asked.

"I think that you may need to put that entire situation to rest," Morgan replied with her usual lack of emotion. "And if you can do so, then I think I know somebody who would step in and assume the role of the regional Psychic."

"And I am guessing that this person would be a friend or ally of yours." It was not a question.

I knew Morgan well enough to be certain that she was always thinking two or three moves ahead. With Templars wanting me gone and the Psychic Council supposedly trying to push Morgan out, things had all the feelings of an encroaching war. Only, I had no idea what that would actually mean in the Supernatural realm.

Sure, I was confident that there would not be large battles fought in the streets since the Supernatural community liked to stay under the radar of mortals, but I was willing to bet that it was at least as unpleasant, if not more so when it came to the levels of violence that would be exhibited.

"Your guess is correct, but I will need you to ensure her safety and eliminate the current Psychic. Afterwards, you will have to assume the title and then lose in battle so that you forfeit the region."

That statement hung in the air for a moment, and at first, I was not entirely sure that I heard her correctly. The whimper from Nose Wart snapped me back to the situation and confirmed that I had not suddenly had my super-seeker hearing go on the fritz.

"Umm…say what?"

"Which part are you unclear about?" Morgan said, sounding as cool as the other side of the pillow.

"Well, I am guessing that I have to kill the current Psychic to assume his role, we already had that talk. My confusion sort of lies in the part about me losing in battle so that I forfeit the region and this little pal of yours takes over."

Well, isn't that interesting, Blodwen sniffed.

Jeez, can't you people stay where I put you? I huffed inwardly.

Blodwen was some sort of ancient creature known as a gwyll. Her full name is Blodwen Cadwallader, Queen of the Celtic Mulingar Gwyllion, Holder of the Blue Sphere, Cosantóir of the Ten Sidhe, but her friends can just call her Muffy. She is some relation to faeries, and having her rambling around in my mind is proving to be more helpful than any of the other residents. She actually takes the time to talk and explain things to me when they fly over my head, which, if you are just joining the party and have missed my previous exploits, happens quite often.

"If I lose to this friend of yours, then I seem to miss the part about how this helps me considering the fact that I would be dead," I sniped at Morgan. Seriously, who did she think she was dealing with? I know I am often the last one to arrive at the solution party, but that does not mean I am a complete idiot.

"Who said anything about you having to die?" Morgan replied, her emotions pegging zero on the meter as always.

"Well, since I have to kill Claude to take him out and assume his position, then I am assuming—" I began, but Morgan cut me off.

"You are not too far removed from your time as a human to remember that old saying about when you assume things." Morgan sipped her tea and continued to gaze at me with that creepy way she has where you just know her eyes are going to dry up and turn to raisins if she doesn't blink. Yet…she never does!

"Okay, then would you mind telling me how I avoid being

killed? Am I supposed to stage my death and go into some sort of Supernatural witness protection program?"

"That is just silly." Morgan gave me a dismissive wave. "Why would you have to fight to the death? And as much confidence as I have in Kari to handle things as the new Dallas Psychic, I doubt she would fare well if she went up against you in a fight."

"Okay..." I let that word drag for a few beats and gave my hands a roll to encourage her to please explain.

Morgan explained and I actually smiled.

That Ghoul Ava on a Roll!

2

So Emotional

"You really think this is a good idea?" Lisa Jenkins sat on my bed as I scrounged through my drawers and closets trying to find clothes that fit me good this month.

What, you think that just because I'm a ghoul I don't still have days when I feel fat? Supernaturals aren't all posterized pretty girls and boys with perfect figures and toned abs; that is just Hollywood and its infinite desire to make regular people feel frumpy, but don't get me started on that right now.

"I think it is a job. I think the pay day is going to be freaking epic, and I think you and I could use some time to deal with our own personal crap away from the other so we don't feel like we have to explain every little thing we do." Yep, I thought, that summed it up just fine.

Lisa Jenkins is my best friend in the world. However, just as it is with every other part of my life, there are some gnarly complications. The biggest would be the fact that Lisa is a Templar...or training to be one—Hell, I've lost track—and the Templars are like the sworn enemy of all ghoul-kind. They apparently tried to completely eradicate the ghouls from existence way back in the olden days.

They failed.

To add to this drama, I guess being a female ghoul comes

with a whole scary skill set that makes them an even bigger threat. The denizens living in my head are proof of that. Again, if this your first excursion into my world, then you have missed out on a lot. I can somehow absorb certain powerful Supernaturals into my being where some version of them lives in my head and can actually talk with me. I also apparently take on some of their abilities that they possessed in the physical world.

Currently, I have Blodwen, who I sort of told you about already; Cody, some kid who apparently has necromantic powers and can create a type of zombie; Butt Pimple, the chosen mate to my little goblin friend, Nose Wart, Mystify, some sort of inhuman thing that I have locked away very securely—at least for now—that might have been the Psychic in Dallas (that part is still a bit fuzzy); and, last but not least, Adrianna, the former and self-professed Queen of the Zombies. All she did was start that whole Black Plague thingy, but apparently the Templars and Augustines worked really hard to sanitize the facts so that it was blamed on rats.

Oh yeah, my world is crazy, and the beauty is that I now get to have my dear ghost writer (yep, an actual ghost who goes by the name of Chantal) jot all of this stuff down in book form for you to pick up just like so much of the other supposed fiction you read that is put out there by other Supernaturals. Hey…a girl has to make a living. Of course, if I relied on this as my sole source of income, I'd be sleeping behind a Dumpster.

"Ava!" Lisa tossed me a blouse that she obviously thought would look good on me and I held it up as I stood in front of the mirror. "I don't need to be away from you to handle my business. Besides, this sounds like a job that has a potential to get ugly. You need back-up, and then there is the whole situation where you need to feed every twelve hours. You need somebody to ensure that you are supplied."

"And I have it."

Almost on cue, Nose Wart skittered into my room with an actual red polka-dotted bandana stuffed with whatever he had decided to bring along hanging from a stick and slung over his shoulder. He was like a Supernatural caricature of an old timey hobo.

"Seriously?" Lisa glared at the little goblin that stopped in his tracks and then bared his teeth at the Templar. He might be terrified of me, but other than that, he, like all goblins, was absolutely fearless.

"I serve Just Ava, and remain at her side to the death. Can you make that same assurance, *Templar*?" the goblin challenged, and the way he said the word 'Templar' was dripping with disdain.

"Ease down there, killer," I said, giving the little goblin a scratch behind one of his leathery ears.

"As you command, Just Ava."

That comment actually made Lisa smirk just a bit. Nose Wart and the goblins actually thought my name was Just Ava after I had corrected some serious groveling in the early days. You know how somebody will call you Mister This or Missus That and you tell them to call you just whatever your name is? Yeah, well the goblins took it literally, and apparently correcting them at this point would bring on great shame or some such nonsense.

I gave the neatly folded clothes in my suitcase a quick once-over and then zipped it shut. I set it beside my door and barely even noticed the huge, furry paw that I was pretty sure belonged to one of the bugbears as it reached in and plucked my stack of luggage to carry it to the car.

"I actually do have something that I could use your help with in my absence." I debated on this one. It might cause some friction between Lisa and me, but I am lousy at filtering out bad choices. "I need you to talk to Belinda for me. If you want somebody to be mad at over this little trip, be mad at her. Apparently one of her Texas vampire pals was given my info which is what led to me being contacted for this job." I let that hang for a second before continuing and then told her about Hector and his human thrall, how Brandy was the thrall's sister and that Belinda sort of offered me up as the solution. I left Morgan's part in things out of the story since that might distract Lisa from my real purpose.

I knew that she was somehow, and for an unknown reason, meeting up with Belinda. In case you missed the memo, she is Queen of the Kiss in the area and sort of my enemy. Not that we have gone at each other, but we are so not ever going to be friends.

"I can look into that," Lisa agreed.

"Also, there is the whole deal with the fake Templars and that stupid ray gun or whatever the hell it is that they shot me with to cause this problem in the first place."

"Already ahead of you on that one," Lisa said, her lips pressing tight as she looked to be warring with a frown that wanted to crease her face. "Edward and Race are in Salem right now tracking down a lead."

"Together?" I asked, just a little curious.

Edward Losli is one of the Supreme Psychics. Not that I really know what that means exactly, but I do know he is part of the Psychic Council. The Psychic Council is the group that wants Morgan out of the picture, but supposedly Mr. Losli does not share their desires and at least appears to be siding with Morgan.

Then there is Race Mitchell. He is a Templar and as far as I know, the one in charge of Lisa's training. He should be my sworn enemy, but he seems to be sort of on my side in things.

Add in the fact that he is super dreamy...who am I kidding! They are BOTH simply hunk-a-licious, and I may someday end my drought of nookielessness.

So, are you confused yet? If not, could you give me a call and explain it to me? I feel like a puppy chasing its tail.

"I guess," Lisa shrugged. She was trying to act like it was no big deal, but I could see in her eyes that she was just as intrigued by this sudden alliance as me.

It isn't like Templars and Psychics are enemies, but Templars are sort of the Supernatural equivalent of the CIA. They are usually poking around in our business and do not seem to have any qualms about staging uprisings and coups to further whatever agenda it is that they have going. They even have a special place where they research weaknesses of the various types of creatures in the Supernatural community and construct weapons to eradicate them.

Psychics are like our guardians and guides. They know every Supernatural in their district and apparently help them fit in to the community. Of course I was never given much help in that regard, but Morgan had her reasons and I have learned to understand them…sort of…a little.

To know that a Psychic and a Templar were working together was one thing. To know that they were doing so on my behalf was mind-boggling. It would be like a tiger and a cheetah working together to save an antelope. Granted, I am a bad-ass antelope, but still…those two would be the least likely candidates to be involved in trying to help keep me safe.

"Oh," Lisa piped up, sounding like she had totally forgotten something very important, "Betty called."

Yeah, I guess that would fall under the category of pretty important. I still don't really know Betty's story, but she is one tough old bird, and capable of all sorts of crazy magic stuff. I know that is a pretty lame description, but I still don't really know what she can do…or can't do for that matter.

The only reason that I knew the treatments that Morgan was getting were tied to her is because Morgan had actually told me. At the moment, Betty was supposedly overseas trying to rally some Supernaturals to our cause…whatever that was.

"How is she?" I asked, trying not to sound too anxious, but in just the short time she had been gone, I was beginning to realize how much I sort of depended on her. She had been instrumental in helping me understand about myself early on, and she also made a good buffer between me and Morgan.

"I guess she has run into another ghoul." That sentence hung in the air with a heavy ominousness that almost felt like a physical presence. "Some guy by the name of Kurt Von Guster. I guess he will be coming here to Portland in the next few days."

I think I sprained my neck whipping my head around that fast. "Say what!"

My first thought was that Morgan was getting me out of town on purpose. There was no way that Betty was sending a ghoul to Portland without telling Morgan. Plus, Morgan would detect the presence of any Supernatural that entered her territory.

"You think they are trying to pull something on you?" Lisa asked, obviously reading the feelings etched on my face.

"I think that I need you here keeping an eye on things now more than ever," I admitted. Lisa smiled, and I saw a tear well up in her eye.

Crap, I thought, *what have I done now?*

"Is something wrong?" I blurted.

"What?" Lisa sniffed and scrubbed at her eyes. "This? No, actually, I am just so… happy."

"Okay?" I sort of drew that word out, my pitch rising just a bit to imply a question.

"We've just drifted apart so much these past several weeks," Lisa said as she wiped at her eyes that were now leaking tears in a steady stream. "I was beginning to think that we might never get back to the way things used to be."

I opened my mouth a few times, but nothing came out. I'd been having those same concerns for a while, but it was as if everything bad from the past was washing away; at least when it came to me and Lisa. I had no idea what a burden that concern had actually been until this precise moment.

I threw open my arms and gave just the slightest nod. Lisa took the cue and jumped to her feet and dove into me. We hugged and there was a lot of blubbering and "I'm sorry" "No, I'm sorry" type stuff going on that I won't bore you with.

When it was done, I looked around the room and was actually surprised to see that not only was Nose Wart still standing where I had last remembered seeing him, but he was joined by several other goblins who all had an assortment of weapons drawn like they were expecting a fight. Among the group was the little goblin formerly known as Twiggle. He'd earned his clan name and was now called Belly Ulcer. I called him Lefty on account of his having no left hand any more due to it being eaten away by acidic lamia blood.

"Shall we open her belly and let you feast on her innards?" Belly Ulcer growled, brandishing a rusty looking clawed and spiked weapon that reminded me of an evil cousin to the Garden Weasel.

"Why would I want you to do that?" I sniffed, actually stepping between Lisa and the goblins.

"She has caused you obvious distress, Just Ava," Belly Ulcer replied with a cold sneer that was actually a little scary sounding.

"What makes you think she has caused me distress?"

"You were obviously overcome," Nose Wart said, shooting a rather hard glare in Belly Ulcer's direction. I had a feeling some sort of goblin protocol was being broken.

I had no desire to explain myself or what was happening between me and Lisa. I stood up straight and fixed the entire little gaggle of goblins with what I hoped was my most regal stare.

"You will not harm Lisa Jenkins under penalty of death and great displeasure. Is that perfectly clear?" I leaned forward just a bit as I spoke, bending at the waist to put my face that much closer to theirs.

It was as if somebody had pulled the plug on the entire bunch. Immediately they were all on their bellies; each one groveling for mercy and forgiveness.

"Enough!" I snapped, cutting the entire pack off in mid-grovel. "Now gather the troops in the backyard. I don't have long before the stupid sun comes up. I need to make sure everybody knows what is going on."

There was a scrabbling of claws on hardwood flooring, and then the room was empty except for me and Lisa. I turned back to face her and saw that she had taken the brief interlude to wipe her eyes and scrub at her face so that her mascara made her look like a raccoon.

"I'm glad we had the chance to say this stuff before I left," I admitted.

"Me too, but I want to go on record as saying that I think I should be at your side for this little mission."

Lisa and I headed to the backyard and it might sound corny, but my steps actually felt lighter. People can say what they want about how strong and independent they are, but I believe that nobody—human or Supernatural—is made to exist without having somebody or something that they can rely on.

Lisa Jenkins has told me over and over that she has my back through thick and thin. I believe her. And the feeling is mutual. We might argue and fight every once in a while, but no relationship I've ever heard of has *not* endured some rocky times. In fact, I would be as bold as to suggest that it is the rough times that help define as well as strengthen any relationship worth a damn.

I stepped out onto my back porch and was actually stunned. I knew that I'd been attracting a variety of creatures over the past several months. What I had not realized was just how many! Seeing them all gathered in one spot was a bit intimidating. Not that I was afraid of any of these creatures, but I was about to speak to them. I am not much when it comes to public speaking and certainly not in front of large crowds. There were well over three hundred assorted Supernaturals standing in my large backyard and that was not counting the few dozen wisps of light that I knew to be pixies flitting about the edge of the pine trees that scrolled out in nice, neat rows.

I scanned the gathering and was surprised to discover two huge Great Danes sitting at doggy attention at the base of the steps leading to my back porch. Even more surprising was the fact that Nose Wart was apparently having a conversation with one of them.

"Rex?" I said.

"Yes?" One of the dogs' heads popped up, but the answer came in stereo and my head swung to the left at the dog then to the right towards the dark shape sitting on the rail that ran along the length of my porch.

Lisa's gargoyles were apparently among the attendees. I'd really only met one of the strange, stony looking things. He'd explained that his name was too difficult for the human tongue and accepted my calling him Rex. One of the Great Danes, the one who had introduced himself to me as Dredge, had explained that his humans called him by that same name. Well, I could clear that up in a hurry.

"You are Dredge when you are in my presence, I will not call you by that other name. And since I have not had the pleasure, who is your friend?" I nodded to the other massive canine.

"My name is Gortch," the dog said with pride. "And I will not reduce myself by giving you the ridiculous name bestowed by the cruel bitch and her weak sire."

"Nice to make your acquaintance, Gortch," I said with a nod.

I would ask later just why exactly the two dogs were in attendance. For now, I had to speak to my little clan and then dismiss everybody before the sun rose. I wasn't the only one who might have adverse reactions to daylight.

"I will be leaving for a while to tend to something in Texas," I began. "In my absence, Lisa Jenkins will be in charge of things here. If you have any issues or problems, you will see her to have it dealt with. Her word will be law, and you will consider any order or request issued by her to be from me as well."

I glanced over at Lisa and was once again amazed at how calm and in control of herself she appeared. I tried to imagine myself at her age and having not only all the knowledge of the Supernatural world, but the whole thing about being a Templar tossed on like an extra helping of poop on an already overloaded poop sandwich.

"Can we ask the nature of this Texas trip?" a voice called from the back of the crowd.

I strained to try and discern which of those gathered might have asked. There were simply too many creatures here, and I was not familiar enough with all their voices at this point. And honestly, so many of these things made sounds that were closer to rumbles and growls than actual speech that I might never be able to do little more than know what sort of creature was speaking.

"I will be dealing with some possible Valkyries," I finally said, seeing no reason to keep it a secret.

The ripple of astonished murmurs that coursed through my little flock actually caught me by surprise. *Great*, I thought, *it sounds like I may have a tougher task ahead of me than I initial-*

ly realized.

"And how will you be travelling to Texas?" another voice that was at least partially familiar asked.

I was surprised to look down and see three beautiful female figures standing just to the left of my stairs. Rain and a pair of her faeries had obviously decided to attend my little briefing.

Rain is the new Godmother of a local Sidhe. Our relationship is…complicated. Due to my having consumed Blodwen, I could technically enter the Sidhe any time I wish, but I have made a promise not do anything of the sort. I gave that vow in the Heart of the Sidhe, so supposedly, it is a binding agreement. I have no desire to test what might happen if I went against that vow more because I don't want to alienate the faeries or turn them hostile towards me.

"I will book a flight for late this afternoon and have Lisa transport me and Nose Wart to the airport in a sealed container," I replied.

"Before you leave, I would have you visit me in my chambers. I believe that I have something that will be of assistance," Rain said.

I was caught between being thankful for her assistance and being so amazed at how sultry her voice could be when she was speaking of something so mundane. Faeries were basically concentrated sexuality when it came right down to it.

Rain had amazingly lustrous, ruby red hair. And this was no color anybody could simply find in a bottle. Her violet eyes sparkled and seemed to suck in all the light around her and then reflect it. She was maybe a shade over five feet tall and her body would shame any Playboy Bunny. It was perfectly symmetrical and a white that was so pale that it verged on blue in its hue. The sheer clothing she was currently wearing left absolutely nothing to the imagination and allowed you to see her mommy parts. A perfect triangle of ruby red in the cleft between her legs seemed to be drawing the gaze of every male goblin; and they were actually drooling.

"Nose Wart!" I hissed when I glanced down at my side and saw the little guy just as guilty of staring as the others under his command.

Do not scold him, Ava, Butt Pimple's voice chirped inside my head. *He is goblin.*

She said that like it was the only explanation that was necessary. Thankfully, Blodwen was on hand.

Goblins are a very virile race. They are not ashamed in any way about their sexuality and staring is actually a compliment in their culture. They are showing honor to the Godmother in their appreciative gaze while also expressing their respect by not acting on their…obvious…desires, Blodwen explained.

I did a double-take; the state of arousal that Rain was creating in the little goblin males was visibly clear. I was really trying my best to fold in to the Supernatural community. I was often accused of maintaining too much of my humanity. It was always said like it was a bad thing; maybe it was, but I could not help who I was or how my mind worked.

"I would be honored to appear as your guest," I replied to Rain.

Just that quick, she and her two-faerie entourage melted into the crowd and disappeared. I scanned the crowd and did not see any of the others seeming to have any questions.

"Okay then," I called out, clapping my hands for emphasis, "that is all. You are dismissed."

I watched as all the assorted creatures that were now calling this former Christmas tree farm their home scurried off to wherever it was they went during the day. I noticed the goblins still hanging around as well as the two massive hounds. Something told me that there might be an issue here. I did not have long to wait to discover exactly what.

That Ghoul Ava on a Roll!

3

Bark at the Moon

"Dredge," Nose Wart yipped, stepping past me as his fellow goblins crowded around, "you have answered my call and now we shall attend to our grudge. This will be finished before I depart with Just Ava. I will not leave my subjects to deal with you and your..." He swung his head in an exaggerated manner to regard Gortch. "You are not a mated pair. So what is your purpose?"

I did not want two dogs butchered in my back yard, but I could not step in and interfere. Butt Pimple was warning me of doing anything at this moment, saying that, if I were to step in, Nose Wart could lose prestige amongst his fellow goblins. The thing is, I had no doubt as to what the outcome would be if a confrontation took place between the two great Danes and this little tribe. The dogs would not stand even the most remote of chances.

"We are litter mates," Dredge said in his growly voice. "We were stolen by the bitch and her lazy sire."

I was now almost certain that the big dog was not using the word "bitch" in a reference to her canine gender equivalent. I could hear the disdain in its words. This was really strange. I mean, I sort of understood how and why I could understand monsters. I imagined that we were all tied together through some

27

sort of Supernatural bond. That did not explain why I could speak the language of dogs.

Yes, Blodwen agreed with my sentiment (apparently I had been projecting that thought inward because the residents in my head were not actually privy to my thoughts), *that is a rather curious development.*

"Stolen?" Nose Wart scoffed. "You allowed those useless scrapings from between the toes of a shit troll to steal you?"

"We were just pups at the time and had little knowledge of what was occurring," Gortch barked defensively.

I sort of took it that Gortch was not quite as bright as his sibling. He sounded like maybe he'd been dropped on his little puppy head at some point. Also, Dredge was dealing with this entire situation with a visible degree of calm. If he was in any way frightened or intimidated by the pack of goblins surrounding him and his brother with weapons drawn and sort of pointed at the massive Danes, there was no indicator. Gortch, on the other hand, was visibly nervous, his tail almost tucked between his legs and the fur at the base of his neck standing on end.

"You are not pups now," one of the other goblins challenged. "Why not simply do away with the humans and take back your freedom?"

Nose Wart spun to the goblin that had spoken and struck with a vicious backhand that sent the little guy staggering on his heels. I instantly recognized the missing hand and knew the offender to be Belly Ulcer.

They will fight to the death soon, Butt Pimple murmured. *The little goblin has allowed his being awarded his tribal name as well as his role in your escaping the belly of that lake troll to cloud his senses.*

To the death? I sighed. *Does it have to be to the death? Can't you guys just have it out in a boxing ring or the Octagon?*

There is only one way for this to end, Butt Pimple replied with finality.

Nose Wart returned his attention to the two Great Danes and planted his hands on his hips. He took a single step forward that put him standing just under the jowls of Dredge. Looking up, he spoke with a calmness and confidence that was sort of impressive. Seriously, if I was mere inches away from the gaping jaws of a creature that looked as if it might be able to gobble me up in one or two bites, I might not be nearly so bold.

"You will cease using our land for your waste elimination." It was not a request.

"I will concede to that wish," Dredge answered.

"It is not a request or wish. It is an edict. To violate it will end this truce I am declaring and result in your death at my hands."

I winced at that statement, and was waiting for blood to spill, but the Great Dane simply dropped his head below Nose Wart's chin and made a whimper that sounded more than a little odd coming from such a large dog. Nose Wart rose up on his tiptoes and gave Dredge a scratch behind one ear.

There was a chorus of hoots and snorts, and then all of the goblins converged on the pair of dogs to pat, stroke, and scratch them. Also, much like when regular dogs meet and greet one another, there was an incredibly gross amount of butt sniffing. Like a pack of...well...wild dogs...the group would spontaneously erupt into a series of yips and howls at the sky. I glanced up and saw only a sliver of a waning moon still visible.

I waded out of the commotion and noticed Belly Ulcer standing just a little ways outside the scene. I was still learning a lot about goblins, but I knew enough of their expressions to see anger seething across his eyes as he apparently refused to partake in the ceremony or whatever it was that was taking place in my yard.

"Is there a reason you are not over there with your fellow goblins?" I asked as casual as I could as I came to stand beside the angry little creature.

"Those beasts fouled our land on numerous occasions. There should be no truce, they should simply be eliminated," Belly Ulcer snarled. He glanced up and suddenly seemed to remember who he was speaking to and immediately flopped onto his stomach.

"Oh get up," I snapped before he could begin begging for

mercy. "And I want to know right now if you are going to be a problem."

The young male goblin looked up at me as he rose to his feet. There was not the fervent glimmer of absolute hate in his beady little eyes, but I could still see anger simmering just below the surface.

"I will never be a problem, Just Ava. I shall serve with absolute loyalty and give all of my being in that service." The goblin made a sweeping gesture with his hands that ended in an awkward looking bow. I had to guess that he'd seen that someplace or something, but it was very obvious that it was not an action that came naturally or with any degree of comfort to him.

"If you truly wish to serve me, then I would have you join in whatever it is that your fellow goblins are doing over there with the two dogs." I folded my arms across my chest and hoped that I was giving the impression of commanding.

"As you wish, Just Ava."

Belly Ulcer turned and walked stiffly to the frolicking and sniffing taking place just a few yards away. I saw him visibly tense as soon as one of the dogs made initial contact, but I noticed him do the same when a few of his fellow goblins touched him as well. Something just seemed off with the little beast.

I turned and headed inside. I was letting the screen door close behind me when I felt a breeze at my back. On instinct, I spun, both my hands already sporting switchfingers.

"Aren't you out a little late?" I snapped at the face staring in at me through the screen door.

The too-pretty face of vampire—and as close to a sworn enemy as something could be without us actually coming to blows—Belinda Yates stared in at me. Her pert, pretty little mouth actually twitched in what might have been her version of a smile.

"Invite me in, please," Belinda said. Her hair was loose and uncharacteristically disheveled, looking like spun white gold wreathing her perfectly oval face. I don't think I'd ever seen her with her hair completely down. I hated how she could look pretty even with her hair obviously (albeit oddly) messy.

"I don't have time for you right now." I gave a dismissive wave and started to shut the door.

"Ava...please!"

I froze. She was almost pleading. If there was any one thing that I would never expect, it would be the scenario that seemed to be playing out at this exact moment on my back porch. I turned and looked into those dead doll eyes that normally regarded me with open disgust. What I saw in the split second it took her to obviously try and compose herself in an attempt to hide how desperate she must be was what, if I did not know better, had to be a look of fear.

"Come in." I stepped back to allow her to enter my kitchen while still keeping what I considered to be a minimum safe distance in case this was some peculiar trick.

I was about to ask what she could possibly be thinking by coming to my house this close to dawn when there was clearly no likely place for her to shelter from the sun before it rose when something else caught my attention. The racket in my back yard that were the goblins and Great Danes partaking in whatever strange ritual they'd begun after agreeing on a truce ended abruptly. In the second it took for me to register that bit of information, the silence turned to snarls and fierce barking.

"Noooo!" Belinda moaned.

Okay, now I was officially unnerved. I felt my control evaporate and my toes went switch to match my fingers before I could kick off my favorite pair of Doc Martens.

"Damn!" I cursed and knew instantly that I'd also gone Sharkmouth.

"You can't hide inside that little house, vampire!" a woman's voice called in a sing-songy way that was very much on the verge of crazy sounding. All she needed to do was chant "Warriors, come out to play-yay!"

I went to the door, actually having to nudge Belinda aside as I passed her. For the first time I knew of, the vampire was obviously scared. Just as my hand touched the handle, the sound of something behind me caused me to spin around. I was just about to slash, but quickly recognized Lisa. She was all decked out in her Templar gear which still reminded me a little too much of some teenaged boy's wet dream of what most female fantasy heroes looked like.

"Who the hell is that in our back yard?" the girl asked. Not "What is one of your most hated Supernaturals doing in your kitchen?" This was more than just a little bit interesting.

"I was just about to go outside and find out," I replied.

"Well don't," Lisa said as she grabbed my arm and pulled me back. In the same instant, she drew a slender blade from a sheath on her left thigh. "One of them has what looks a lot like that ray gun thingy you described those renegade Templars as packing when they tried to take you out in Tillamook."

"But they are after Belinda." I hiked a thumb over my shoulder at the vamp which had been uncharacteristically quiet this whole time.

"Still," Lisa pushed open the screen door and let it slam behind her, "I want you to stay put at least for a moment." Without another word she bounded away from the door and at an angle that took her from my line of sight.

A yelp sounded from outside and I could not tell if it was one of the Great Danes or one of my goblins. In any case, Lisa had another thing coming if she thought that I was just going to stay put. I yanked the screen door open so hard that it came free from the hinges. I would be billing whoever the hell this was in my yard for the damages…if they survived.

I thought I was ready for whatever might be waiting in my backyard…I wasn't.

I immediately recognized the outfits, although I could not be certain they were the same people who had attacked me in Tillamook. They were decked out in Templar battle attire and not one, but two of them had those nasty ray guns. I watched as a ball of energy rolled across my backyard and slammed into one of the goblins. The tiny creature never knew what hit it as it was enveloped in a bright blue flash and then basically disintegrated with its death howl fading as it became an outline of dust for just a second before being whisked away on the morning breeze.

I shot a wary glance to the east and could detect just the

slightest glow of the sun that would be rising soon. If I was going to help, I needed to work fast. That meant this could not be pretty.

In a single leap, I was standing beside one of the renegades holding one of the cursed weapons of Supernatural destruction. In a single swipe I took the head off. It wasn't until the severed head came to a stop face up that I even registered that this one had been a woman. I heard Lisa shout something, but I was in the early throes of what I had to imagine to be some sort of battle lust.

I spun, seeking the bearer of the second ray gun and managed to dive to the side as one of those balls of energy whizzed past my left shoulder, missing me by a fraction of an inch. Once again I leaped and this time I aimed for the area right behind this intruder. My feet barely touched the ground and I was about to swipe at my intended target when I got a bit of surprise in the form of a mule kick to the gut. Apparently this guy was in no mood to let me just end his life quick and clean like I had his comrade.

The next surprise came when he spun on his heel and brought his weapon up to bear. There was no way that he could miss at this range and I briefly wondered if I would disintegrate like the little goblin had just a few seconds ago.

A loud howl caught my would-be executioner off guard and he flinched just enough so that his shot went right over my head. From his left, a tiny figure had sprung and hit just under the arm outstretched and holding the weapon.

"Die, human!" the goblin snarled.

I watched as Nose Wart drove the small blade he carried up and under the chin of the man, the point exploding through the top of the man's head in a gout of blood and gooey gray matter. He yanked his weapon free and rode the man's dying body to the ground, stabbing him in the chest at least twice before they landed.

I rolled away and surveyed the situation. Three of the renegades lay dead or dying, and two more were trying to fend off a very angry pack of goblins. Lisa had one of the intruders pinned against the black van that they had apparently arrived in.

Just as fast as it had begun, this fight was over. Three goblins were sprawled in the grass, adding to the carnage and one of the Great Danes was limping, its right rear leg tucked up against its body. I couldn't tell which one, and for some reason, that bothered me. These dogs had just risked their lives defending my home against a renegade attack and I didn't even know which one was Dredge and which one was Gortch.

"We lost three to these terrible weapons," Nose Wart said from beside me.

I glanced down and saw dark blood dripping from his chin. He was holding the weapon by the tip of the handle like a squeamish new parent might hold that first dirty diaper. And don't ask me why that comparison came to mind...I have no idea. I took the weapon, and when I could not find anything that looked like a safety, I just held it pointed skyward.

"Ava!" Lisa's voice shouted with urgency.

My head snapped around and I saw her trying to fend off a pack of angry goblins that had closed in and were now gathered in a semi-circle. They didn't want her; they wanted the lone survivor that remained of our assailants. I was tempted to let them have the bastard, but I had the presence of mind to know that a survivor might yield answers.

"Everybody inside!" I ordered.

Almost as one, I saw the goblins turn to face me. It was clear that they were not happy with my order, but they did not even consider disobeying. They trooped inside, some of them actually having the stones to cast a dirty look my way as they passed.

I looked down at Nose Wart. "Call the bugbears and have them move the bodies to my freezer." Hey, a ghoul's gotta eat.

I stomped over to Lisa and her captive. This one was a man and he was eyeing me with very obvious hatred and disgust. He looked like a man in his early thirties, but with a Templar, it is sort of hard to tell an actual age since they have those rings that seem to halt the aging process.

"You won't escape us all," the man spat in lieu of an actual greeting; not that I expected one.

"Yes, well, you won't be the one to ring the bell," I shot back. "But you weren't after me to begin with. You were chasing a vampire. Care to tell me why?"

"She is an abomination…one of the undead, and therefore, must be purged."

I was actually surprised that I'd received any answer at all. This was not the first time I'd heard these sorts of statements. Maybe I was their Public Enemy Number One but it sounded to me like there was a bigger picture here.

"You disgust me!" Lisa snapped, yanking the man around by the wrists and bringing him to his knees in one deft movement that elicited a little bark of pain.

The man, despite being several inches taller and at least a hundred pounds heavier, made no move to resist. Whether it was me in full on switchdigit-mode with Sharkmouth in effect, the goblin with crimson drool dripping from his chin who was now directing a handful of bugbears—basically seven-plus foot tall gremlin-looking beasts with coarse hair and mouths lined with some nasty, razor-sharp fangs—as they dragged the corpses of his former companions to my house, or the trio of jötunn that had emerged from the trees with clubs over their shoulders that were longer than this man was tall, he made the prudent choice to submit.

"Get him inside," I said as I headed for the door. I did not want it to look as if I was desperate, but in the short time that had elapsed during this little scuffle, the sun had reached the horizon and its light seemed to race across my property in an attempt to scorch me before I could retreat to safety.

I did not even pause as I headed for the basement. I was a little surprised to discover Belinda sitting on my light-proof box that I'd been transported in more than once and would be using in just a few hours to make the trip to Texas.

"I hate to impose," Belinda said with what I guess passed as a smile for her.

It took me a moment to first come to grips that she was conscious. Most vampires simply died when the sun rose. It was their weakness and the reason that many lesser vamps had humans that attended to and kept watch over them during daylight hours. The bigger issue was how polite she was being. If you know anything about my relationship with this particular vampire, then you are probably just as confused.

"Oh, this must absolutely suck for you," Lisa chuckled as she escorted our prisoner to a metal chair in the corner and began tying him down.

Belinda shot Lisa a glare, but she quickly wiped it from her face and attempted to paste that smile back on. When the situation fully dawned on me, I had to fight to suppress an all-out snort of laughter. Belinda was completely at my mercy. I knew from a previous incident that if I revoked my invitation, she would be flung from my house. With the sun up, I was pretty certain that she would not stand a chance. Sure, she might be able to resist the sleep/death that less powerful vamps endure, but there was absolutely no way that she could withstand the power of the sun.

"You want to tell me what happened?" I asked. I didn't need to clarify, she knew perfectly well what I was referring to; how had she ended up at my doorstep with renegade Templars on her heels.

"If I tell you, will you give me your word that you will not get defensive and revoke my invitation?" Belinda asked.

Wow, if I wasn't curious before, Blodwen murmured from someplace in my head.

"I promise." I am a lot of things. Hell, I might even have moments when I can be petty, but the way I saw it, Belinda was currently under my protection.

"I was just leaving the residence of a thrall of mine that lives near here. One of my lesser vampire minions was supposed to be waiting out front in his car to take me home. I saw the car and was only a few steps from it when this black van raced around the corner and tried to run me over.

"It was an easy matter to jump out of the way, but unfortunately, my minion was not so lucky. They had slammed into the side of the car and before he could act, they rushed the car and fired one of those horrid weapons at it. The ball of energy, or whatever it is, literally passed right through the window and appeared to disintegrate my poor Grady." Belinda shot a glance over at the renegade that was now firmly bound and gagged in the corner.

I don't even think I blinked, but all of a sudden she was behind the man, her fangs flashing and her lips so close to the man's throat that there would be absolutely no way for me to stop her if she decided to strike. She did not bite the man, but as she resumed her narration, she did not move even a fraction of a centimeter from her position hovering over the man's jugular.

"They started shouting something about atrocities, and then one of them said that I was, and I am basically quoting them here, a known associate of that abomination that is the ghoulish whore, Ava Birch."

"Whore?" I scoffed. "Wow, I don't know who they've been talking to, but I haven't experienced a sexual drought like this since…" I pursed my lips and scrunched my face up as I thought. "Nope…never. I've never gone this long. The last nookie I got was Jeremy."

Belinda's brow twitched and I suddenly wondered if she was actually aware that one of the vamps in her Kiss had been my lover for a brief period. Of course it had not been all that great. I mean, he was just fine as a lover, but a vampire smells like rotten chocolate cake frosted with that sludge that you find at the bottom of a Dumpster; at least they do to a ghoul.

"Yes, well, I knew the sun was coming and I also knew that I could not take those bastards to my lair. I have two young vamps that are currently sleeping in my house and they would be defenseless against any attack."

Hmm, good for Belinda. I was a little embarrassed at how surprised I was that she would consider the well-being of another over her own. You know how it is; if you really dislike somebody, it is hard to see them capable of anything good. Then it came to me!

"So you brought them to *my* house!" I could feel the beginnings of the desire to revoke my invitation starting to build in my gut.

"You are a ghoul," Belinda answered, and it was with a degree of certainty and matter-of-factness that struck me as having a deeper meaning than my growing anger was allowing me to understand.

"Ava!" I heard the warning in Lisa's voice and tried to calm myself before I did something irreversible that I might regret...although I doubted I would regret it for long.

"You are a warrior now, Ava Birch," Belinda explained. It was obvious in her tone that she suddenly realized the precipice from which she was currently dangling. "If anybody stood a chance against these horrible humans, it is you. It proved to be true."

"Tell that to the goblins that died in my backyard!"

"Honorable deaths," Belinda said. My expression must have darkened as my anger started to renew at the cavalier manner in which she was apparently regarding the deaths of my little goblin crew. "Ask them!" she blurted with uncharacteristic pleading that caused her voice to crack.

"She speaks truthfully, Just Ava," Nose Wart spoke from behind me.

His words were echoed almost perfectly in my head by Butt Pimple. However, she continued on to elaborate the point.

Those goblins will be revered for generations, the female goblin explained from her confines within my head. *They gave their lives in battle, against renegade Templars no less. To add to their glory, they served in the protection of their mistress...you as well as the local Queen of the Kiss. Their names will be removed from use for a span of a hundred years as a show of honor and respect. Two of them left behind mates, one of those mates was female and she will immediately be granted the privilege of mating with Nose Wart until she is heavy with a litter.*

I felt my anger starting to recede. My gaze swung to the man tied in his chair who had been listening to all of this. I stalked over to him, ray gun now held in front of me and pointed at the man's chest. I had to give him credit; he was at least giving off the impression that he wasn't scared out of his mind.

"So," I said casually as I stopped in front of my prisoner, "what are we going to do with you?"

That Ghoul Ava on a Roll!

4

Flying High Again

"I'm not afraid of you," the man said when I yanked the gag from his mouth, my finger blades cutting through the cloth like it was melted butter. I looked at his features and decided that he must have some serious Italian heritage in his family tree. He could almost be a spitting image of Carmine Ragusa from *Laverne & Shirley*, and if you have never watched *Laverne & Shirley*...you have my pity.

"You should be." I knelt in front of him and fixed him with my black-eyed gaze. I saw him try to hide the little gulp, but there was nothing he could do to hide the beads of sweat popping up on his temples. His curly dark hair was starting to shine a little, and one curl in particular was already stuck to his forehead. "Do you have any idea who or *what* I am?" I pushed the barrel of the peculiar gun up under his chin to emphasize my point.

"I know that you are an unholy and soulless creature that should not be allowed to exist. I know that you tip the scales of a very delicate balance, and that killing you will help restore that balance." The words rolled of his tongue as if by rote, like it was some sort of mantra that had been burned into his mind so deep that they'd lost meaning. Sort of like *The Lord's Prayer* or *The Star-Spangled Banner*; just words that are said over and over to the point where people stop really thinking about them.

"Okay, that seems to be the general consensus," I conceded. "But what about Belinda? Vampires are much more plentiful and have been around for ages. Why the sudden interest in taking them down?"

"Nice question, Ava," Lisa said with genuine appreciation.

"Thanks." I flashed her a quick smile around Sharkmouth and then returned my focus to the renegade.

"She is in league with you," the man said plainly. "She has her minions patrolling your property, and she is corrupting one of the newest members of our order."

Okay, that last bit was obviously in reference to Lisa. I had my own questions about the private meetings between my friend and one of my most despised enemies, but I had come to terms with the idea that Lisa would let me know if there might be something that pertained to me. I'd finally reinvested all my trust in her, and that had to be absolute. If she met with Belinda, she had her reasons and it was none of my business...unless she really wanted to tell me.

However, there was that first bit about how Belinda supposedly had her minions patrolling my property. Was he confused? Did he think that the goblins were hers? I knew that regular humans could not see my little clan, but that any who might possess true psychic energy and abilities could. That was one of the most basic prerequisites for becoming a Templar according to Lisa. It made sense that you would need to be able to see what you were fighting. Goblins are hideous, but why would he think they served Belinda?

"You better tell her," Lisa prompted. "Best she hears it from you."

"My Kiss has been keeping tabs on your house here and the land surrounding it," Belinda said after shooting daggers from her eyes in Lisa's direction. "We have been under strict orders from Morgan to keep an eye on you since you were tagged by one of those horrible weapons. Where do you think Lisa has been coming up with your regular prescribed dose of a corpse every twelve hours? My people have been tending to that need…in a manner of speaking."

I felt my mouth hanging open and had no idea how long it had been that way as I stared at this vampire. She's had her people keeping watch over me? Supplying me with fresh corpses? I guess I had chosen not to see the signs, but now that I dug up a few memories, I do recall some rather fresh bodies the past few days.

"Hell has a place for the likes of you," the man snarled. The thing is, I had no idea who he was directing that comment at; me, or Belinda. Probably both.

"I think I've had enough of you, and I doubt you will tell me anything useful anyway." I pulled the trigger on the ray gun and watched as the ball of energy hit the man directly in the middle of the chest.

I was not sure what to expect. I'd seen it vaporize my goblins. I know it had hurt me pretty bad, and I'd barely been nicked. What I didn't expect was for it to have absolutely no effect at all.

The man looked down, and then rolled his eyes back up at me, a huge grin spreading across his face like an oil slick. I guess he forgot the part about being tied to a chair with a pissed off ghoul, a vampire, a goblin, and a Templar that was clearly not on the same team that he was playing for all gathered around and each one very capable of ending him in the blink of an eye.

"Those don't work on Templars," the man scoffed. "They are set to resonate at a frequency that disrupts the unnatural."

"And how old would you be?" I shot back. He looked at me with obvious confusion. "I know for a fact that you Templar types wear an enchanted ring that stops your aging process." I glanced down at his hand and snatched the glove from it hard enough that I think I heard a joint or two pop in the process. Who am I kidding? I absolutely heard, felt, and saw the knuckle of his middle and index finger pop out of joint.

"Ava, I think—" Lisa whispered, but I held up a hand to silence her.

"This is between me and The Big Ragu here," I hissed. "You think that living several decades…lifetimes even…that

that makes you normal? I got news for ya, Sunshine, you are just as much of a technical abomination as any vamp, goblin, ghost, or ghoul."

My hand covered his now and I felt the coldness of the ring he wore as a symbol of his service to the Templars. I kept thinking of him as a renegade, but was that accurate? He was actually adhering to their original charter; it was my Lisa and Race who were the real renegades.

That is the funny thing about wars and feuds; both sides feel that they are the righteous ones. Both sides feel like they have been wronged or transgressed against. I don't know of any instance where one side has openly declared that they are the evil villain. That meant that, if somebody was writing this story from the other side, I would be the bad guy...Lisa would be a traitor.

Yeah, well this is my story, so I get to be the one wearing the white hat.

I felt the man's hand tremble slightly when I touched his ring. My head snapped up and I fixed him with my stare once again.

"I'm curious as to just how much of a badass you would be if you didn't have this little ring that healed you, cleansed your body of toxins, and basically stopped you from aging."

The man's eyes went wide. Not just a little flicker of startlement or surprise. Nope, they went so wide that his whites seem to double in size.

"Do it!" Belinda hissed, her mouth still hovering near the man's throat, her fangs scraping his flesh just enough to leave a pair of red welts that ran along the blue cord that pulsed just below the surface where life blood was now pumping at an accelerated rate.

The man clenched his fist as if he actually believed that could keep me from taking his ring if I really wanted to. The funny thing is that I hadn't really and truly wanted to until he made a fist. For whatever reason, that just set me off. I slid one switchfinger into his balled fist, feeling it slice through the meat of his palm like it was nothing.

"Open your hand...or I might just take all your fingers and

leave you four short of being able to count to ten."

"D-d-don't…p-p-please," the man actually stammered. The little beads of sweat were now rivulets, and there could be no doubt that this man was very afraid.

"Oh, now you wanna use manners. Now it's all 'please' and I bet you'd even toss in a 'thank you' if it came down to it," I taunted. I could feel a strange energy welling up from deep inside. My rational mind thought that it felt oily and gross, but the part of me venting this hot anger only saw it as fuel and tried to siphon up more of it from whatever resource it emanated from. "I wonder how long it would take for me to get you to beg for me to kill you," I whispered, shooting a sly wink at my captive.

Hmm, where was this nasty version of me coming from? I am a lot of things, but cruel has never been on the list. I looked up and saw two very opposite expressions that told me where I was on the spectrum of un-Ava-like in my actions. Lisa looked horrified; Belinda looked delighted.

That should have been a clue. Unfortunately, whatever I was under the influence of when it came to my nasty disposition would not let go. The man opened his hand very slowly and I used my index finger and thumb to get a grip in his ring.

I slid it past the first knuckle and the man once again clenched his fist. I felt a low thrum that seemed to be emanating from the ring and almost let go of it. The thing was, a voice in my head (that absolutely did *not* belong to any of the current residents) was urging me to take the ring.

Tread with caution, Ava, Blodwen's voice warned, but it had to compete with whatever it was that urged me towards this cruel nature.

"Ava, I think you need to eat something," Lisa said, her voice coming across clear as a bell.

"Maybe I will," I laughed as I leered at the man tied to the chair.

In a flash, a hand struck me across the face and my head snapped up. To her credit, Lisa did not take a step back, but I did see her flinch.

"This isn't you, Ava. Ava Birch is not a heartless, cold-blooded murderer. You might be a killer…but you are absolutely not a murderer, and that is exactly what you would be doing if you kill this man who is your prisoner." Lisa reached over and touched my arm.

I took her in and realized how much she had changed in the relatively short time she and I had been friends. The scared little girl I met in that hotel room was impossible to find under the fierce eyes that held me fixed at the moment. I'd never paid any real attention before, but she had vibrant hazel-colored eyes that swirled with just a hint of blue. Her strawberry-blonde hair was currently dyed black which I did not feel was a flattering color on her. Only, I realized that it wasn't because it made her any less beautiful; she simply looked more grown up and self-assured.

Was that my problem? Lisa did not actually need me to take care of her. And, when I really thought about it, she was the one who was taking care of me more often than not. She was my…

"Jiminy Cricket," I breathed. In an instant, my fingers and toes reverted to normal and even Sharkmouth faded so fast that I felt my lips change back.

"Excuse me?" Lisa arched an eyebrow at me.

"You're my conscience," I said simply. My gaze returned to the man, and I eased his ring all the way back to where it belonged. "And that means you get to live."

"Are you insane?" Belinda snapped.

I had almost forgotten she was standing right there behind the man in the chair. I saw her fangs move a fraction closer to the man's throat and I cleared mine, giving my head a slight shake. She would have one chance to heed my warning; if she did not, then things could get nasty fast. I was surprised when I realized that I really did not want to end Belinda. (Sure, that could change in five minutes, but at this very second, I was not interested in killing the vampire pain in my ass.)

"I think I am going to leave this guy to you, Lisa." I stepped away and was relieved to see Belinda stand up and come from behind the man who was now apparently my first official prisoner of war. I turned to the vampire and made a slight nod, "And you are welcome to remain here until it is safe for you to leave. Now, if you all will excuse me, I have a trip to get ready for.

***

"Welcome to the Godmother's audience chamber," the young-looking female faerie recited with reverence. She did not look any older than thirteen or fourteen, but since she is a faerie, I don't know how old she might actually be. I do know that no thirteen-year-old human should be dressed in something so flimsy that was practically see-through and left nothing to the imagination.

"Enter, Ava Birch, and be our honored guest," Rain said from her seat on the throne of the Godmother. At each side of the throne was a pair of female faeries, but it was the score of males ringing the room that caught my primary focus.

Each of these males was atop a pedestal that looked like the base a statue might rest upon. The men all had the pommels of what I had to assume to be bladed weapons jutting from behind each shoulder. However, it was the very large bows with arrows nocked in placed and partially drawn, the tips pointed at me and following my progress across the room that were the real concern.

"Umm, Rain?" I heard my voice squeak. I glanced down and was more than a little surprised to see that Nose Wart did not appear even the slightest bit interested in the firing squad tracking our progress as we approached the Godmother.

The faerie stood, and her ruby red hair cascaded down to the floor and pooled at her feet. I did not recall her hair having been so long, but I was really not able to get past all the arrows pointed at me to give it much more than a passing thought.

"Welcome, Ava, ghoul and protector of the New Noel Forest." Rain made a slight nod. Again, I had no clue what the New Noel Forest might be, but I was still unable to do much more than stare at the arrows pointed in my direction.

"Archers, at ease," Rain announced. She stepped down from the dais and reached her hands out to me as I reached her.

Kneel and take her left hand, Blodwen instructed. I did as I was told; a bit miffed that she had let me swing this long before offering any guidance. *Now, recite these words...*

"Glorious Godmother, greeter of the dawn and savior of the New Noel Forest, I am honored to be accepted as your guest and offer you peace." It was a bit disjointed and halting as I had to listen to a few words, recite them, and then get the next few, but at last I made what I assumed to be a formal greeting.

Rain regarded me with an amused smile. "Blodwen Cadwallader, Queen of the Celtic Mulingar Gwyllion, Holder of the Blue Sphere, and Cosantóir of the Ten Sidhe is obviously present in your consciousness." She laughed, but it was not an "at me" laugh, and it actually brought a smile to my lips. "I apologize for having my protectorate retinue present, but the first year can be the most difficult for a new Godmother, and we do live close to you."

I wasn't going to ask a lot of questions, but at least I knew that those archers weren't on display just for my benefit. "So, you asked me to stop in before I left. I have to be at the airport in about an hour so that my crate can be loaded on the plane. You mentioned having something that might help me deal with Valkyries?"

Rain reached inside the sleeve of her gown which looked like it had been spun from fine spider silk. Considering what I was dealing with, I did not discount that as an actual possibility. She presented me with a golden bracelet. It did not look ornate or fancy in any way, but I had a feeling there was (as usual) a lot that I was missing.

That is interesting, Blodwen murmured. *I did not believe that item to even actually exist any longer. I would be willing to bet that was something that belonged to the former Godmother since she is likely one of the only faeries that would have been old enough to have obtained it.*

"This is woven from the hair of Freyja," Rain explained. "If you can get this onto the wrist of the leader of these Valkyries, she will be forced to submit to you."

Now, on the surface, that seemed like a pretty simple task.

Granted, as I said, the bracelet was nothing special, and getting a woman to put on jewelry should be no problem. Right? Yeah, I didn't believe it would be that easy either.

"Anything else that you can say that might make this task easier?" I was hopeful that maybe Rain would have some secret trick up one of those gossamer sleeves.

"Ava, I've just given you something that will exert total control over some of the fiercest warrior women to exist, I doubt I could make this much easier." There was a moment of silence, and then Rain smiled. "I have total faith in you, Ava."

That made one of us.

I thanked her and then asked to be excused in the manner Blodwen described. Nose Wart and I walked along with our guide and when the exit door opened, I was only a step away from my pickup. Lisa was sitting in the driver's seat and hopped out as soon as she saw the doorway. I pulled on my cowl and made certain to remain in the shadows cast by the tall trees that bordered the road where we'd been told to arrive for this little appointment. I hurried to the cargo area and climbed into my light-proof box with Nose Wart.

"What's that?" Lisa pointed to the bracelet I still had in my hand."

"Apparently this is my secret weapon," I said without much conviction.

To her credit, Lisa didn't ask any questions. We headed for the airport and before we'd even managed to put half of just the drive behind us, I was already wondering if I was going to be able to endure the entire journey with my little travel companion.

As a ghoul, I am gifted with an enhanced sense of smell. Only, my sense of smell doesn't work quite like everybody else's. I smell death, but to me, it is absolutely delicious. Up until this point, I guess I'd simply tuned out the funky stench of my little goblins. Between his flatulence (which is very similar to the stink of a skunk) and his normal goblin stink, I was wondering if I might vomit. By the time I heard the engines of the jet wind up and felt us racing down the runway, I was wishing that I could get sick only because I was hoping the reek of my sick would somehow mask the smell of Nose Wart.

"So," I said, trying to get my mind off focusing on the horrible odor that now felt like it was coating my nostrils and the back of my throat with a rancid, oily layer, "we never really talk. I don't know much about you."

"What would you wish to know, Just Ava?" Nose Wart shifted a little and wedged himself into the corner of the box, appearing as comfortable as if he were riding in first class.

"Well, you made a choice when we first met to abandon your people and come join me. Why would you do that?"

"The Cow Fart clan had been without a true leader for decades," Nose Wart said. "We'd been sworn into service of the Psychic Blumegastrickfiggernilly. He is a coward and knows nothing of goblins. He profited by selling entire litters to others who used the little ones for food or sport. While no goblin fears death, we prefer it to be with some degree of honor. Blumegastrickfiggernilly denied us that honor. Sadly, too many of the cowardly Cow Fart clan accepted this life. When you stood up to him, when you showed no fear of the one who called himself our master, I decided that I would happily serve you."

"Just that quick?"

Nose Wart seemed confused by my question. He stared at me with his large eyes, his head tilted in that way he had that made me think of him as a cute little puppy. I felt Butt Pimple stirring and could actually feel her displeasure with the feelings that I must obviously be broadcasting to my mind's inner sanctum.

"It was not quick, Just Ava. It is a choice I made years ago, but simply waited for the right being to come forward and be worthy of that choice," Nose Wart finally answered.

"Do you have any family still back in Tillamook serving Blu?" I changed the subject.

"No, I have no family left in the Cow Fart clan, Just Ava. My family is here now. The Goblin Vomit clan is my family now and forever."

I was about to question him when Butt Pimple spoke up. *He has divorced himself of that past, Ava. Do not try to make human sense of this.*

"Well..." I finally said, "I am glad you are with me now. I hope I never make you feel like you are dishonored...or regret making the choice to follow me."

"I will serve you to my death, Just Ava. You have already earned that. Nothing you could do now can erase your honor."

I opened my mouth to ask him what exactly I'd done; but once again, Butt Pimple was waving me off; insisting that to question his choice would be an insult. He'd made up his mind and my only choices were to accept it or kill him. I thought that to be a little extreme, but I did as I was asked and kept my mouth shut.

So, are you going to be my goblin conscience? I asked the female goblin stalking around inside my mind. *You seem to have a lot to say the past few days about what I should and should not say when dealing with our little Nose Wart.*

I am simply watching out for my sire, and the leader of our clan, the scratchy voice snarled in defiance.

Do you and I have a problem? I shot back. I didn't really like this new development of how Butt Pimple was talking to me.

You may have earned his respect, but I know how you think of not only my Nose Wart, but of all us goblins. You see us as nothing more than disposable pets that serve your bidding when you need fodder for the killing field, and then ignored otherwise. We are not pets like these puppies you keep comparing us to in your mind, we are warriors, proud and fierce. Nose Wart is perhaps one of the bravest of our kind that I've ever encountered. His loyalty to you will be his undoing, and your coddling of him and treating him with human ignorance will only speed that process.

Jeez, don't hold back, Butt Pimple, tell me how you really feel.

Silence. That was all I received. She'd gone and shut herself away, apparently finished with this conversation.

For the remainder of the flight, Nose Wart slept, which apparently brought on a degree of relaxation that increased his occurrences of flatulence. I wished desperately that I could sleep, or maybe block the stench in this box from my senses.

At last, I heard the sounds of the wheels dropping and felt the plane begin its descent. I knew that Lisa had made arrangements for my box to be picked up and delivered to a location that Race had supplied, saying that it was basically a Templar equivalent of a safe house.

Funny, I hadn't really asked anything about exactly where I was being taken. It actually felt good in a funny sort of way to know that I'd been comfortable placing this great of a degree of trust not only in Lisa, but in Race as well.

There was a bit of jostling, but eventually we were loaded on to (or into) a vehicle. The ride was fairly brief which led me to believe that, wherever we'd been taken, it was close to the airport.

I heard something scratch around outside the box, and then the lid was unlocked and popped open. I looked up and felt a smile of disbelief cross my features. I also heard a low growl start deep in Nose Wart's chest; apparently he was just as surprised as I was to see a trio of vampires staring down at us with fangs on display like they were jockeying for a spot at a blood buffet.

5

Too Shy

"You must be Ava Birch," a female said in a voice that was very Texan in its twang.

"Okay, what I would like is for you all to step back so I can climb out of this box," I said as Nose Wart drew the blade at his hip and moved to my side.

"Oh my!" the female vampire exclaimed, actually sounding a bit embarrassed. "Where are my manners? Tish, Devonna, please step back so our guest can get out of that box." The vampire doing all the talking leaned forward just a bit and peered into the box, her nose wrinkled. "Did your goblin get airsick? I can have somebody brought in to clean out the box so that it will be tidy when you return home."

"No, nobody got sick," I groaned as I stood and stretched. Part of that was real; I did need to stretch after being cooped up in that big crate for so long, but the other part was for me to be able to scan the room. I could smell the vile reek that vampires present to ghouls, but I could also smell something else.

Human.

Yummy.

Dead?

My eyes found a body on a metal gurney in the corner. It was covered to the neck, but there was no denying that it was a corpse.

"We have taken the liberty to have something ready for you to eat," the spokes-vampire said with an arm extending to the tasty treat. "I was told that you require a full meal of a fresh human corpse every twelve hours, no exceptions."

"I got the names of your companions, but who are you exactly, and who has told you all of this?" I said as I climbed out of the box and gave Nose Wart a hand so that he could take his place beside me.

"I am such a ninny-head," the female vampire sputtered, sounding a lot like Kathy Bates for just a moment. If she suddenly told me that she was my number one fan, we might have to fight.

"My name is Nancy Belltran, and please forgive my lapse in manners, I've just never met an honest-to-goodness ghoul before, and you come with a bit of notoriety in your purse."

I gave Nancy a good once over. She was sporting some heavily bleached hair that was almost the color of white gold, and kept in twin braids on each side of her head with a little blue bow at the end of each one. She had bright blue eyes and they sat on either side of a perky little nose that I just wanted to tweak! I guessed her to be just a few inches above five feet tall with a bust line that had to put quite a strain on her lower back—basically a Dolly Parton bobble head doll. She was a little thick in the waist which I personally loved. It punched another hole in that glamour girl/pretty boy vampire crap that littered the big and little screen. And the great thing was that she wore every pound with pride. She was rockin' that bod in some cowgirl jeans and a checkered shirt tied at the midriff like a modern day Ellie May...and if you don't know who Ellie May Clampett is...you have my pity.

As for the other two, Tish and Devonna, they were the completion of a male fantasy triumvirate. Tish had shoulder length jet black hair and was easily six feet tall. Her figure was what most people would classify as athletic. I didn't like her. She needed to eat a sandwich or something. She had dark brown eyes that seemed to have no trouble looking down at me past that sharp, Roman nose. I got the impression that she was the dark, brooding type with little to no sense of humor.

Devonna was the least vampirey (is that even a word?) looking of the bunch. She was average height, but well above average in the weight department. She had carrot orange hair that sat on her head like an angry nest of curly snakes. Her eyes were a greenish hazel color that really sparkled and stood out against her white-even-for-a-vampire skin. And talk about freckles! Holy crap, she looked like she mugged Pippi Longstocking for her facial smattering. However, if Nancy was smiling, then this woman was taking it as a personal challenge to have the biggest, goofiest grin in the room. Her eyes kept flitting to Nose Wart and I saw something in her look that had me instantly self-conscious about how I'd been regarding my little goblin contingent. She was looking at him like a little girl might gawk at a puppy in the store window. (Did you just hum "How much is that doggie in the window"?)

Is that what I've been doing? I thought to Butt Pimple, hoping that it would reach her in whatever little room she'd shut herself away in after our last exchange. I was not surprised when I didn't get a response, but looking at Devonna had me making a vow to myself to see my goblins as they are and not try to humanize them. Or is that puppyize? Anyway, you get the idea.

"We were briefed by the Portland Queen of the Kiss as to your...condition. I assure you that we are sworn to secrecy and will reveal nothing of your condition to anybody." Nancy was heading over to the body on the gurney and motioning for me to follow. "It should be a simple matter of providing you with fresh meals in the time frame you require...one of my thralls is a guard at the local prison where a fresh meal is just a phone call away."

"That's handy," I said as I stared down at the body laid out before me. The hint of a poorly done tattoo crept up the side of his neck, and the number "214" was inked on his forehead. "Seems a bit much to have his serial number on his forehead."

"Oh, that's not his serial number, Sugar. That's his local area code. Some of the little gang bangers do that as a show of solidarity or something," Nancy explained.

"Wow…nothing says I don't ever want to be able to get a job again like slapping a tattoo on your forehead," I scoffed as Sharkmouth came and I prepared to toss down the convict-*du-jour*.

For some reason, I suddenly became self-conscious. I was about to devour this body in front of three total strangers; and they were vampires to boot.

"Would you ladies mind excusing me for a few minutes?" I gave a shift of my eyes to the stairs leading up as a bit of a hint.

"Oh! Yes…we'll be waiting in the parlor," Nancy blurted, scooting the other two towards the exit.

I could tell that Devonna was extremely disappointed. Her lower lip stuck out in a pout that had me almost wanting to apologize. I quickly realized that it was not her regret at not being able to watch me feed; her eyes never left Nose Wart as she vanished from sight.

"I think you have an admirer," I said before digging into the yummy treat laid out for me.

Nose Wart started and when I looked down at him, I caught him just as he tore his eyes away from the stairs the trio of vamps had just vanished up. A closer look revealed something even more…interesting.

"Are you gawking at that vampire?" I managed around a mouthful of leg. "Nose Wart's got a girlfriend!" I sing-songed.

"What?" the goblin sputtered. He turned his back to the stairs and the hint of ruddiness in his cheeks that I had taken for blushing was even more visible now that his face was fully bathed in the light of the small bulb that hung from a single cord in the middle of this basement.

"You were giving oogly eyes to that red-haired vampire," I teased.

"That would not be acceptable!" Nose Wart protested; however, those same words were chimed by Butt Pimple as well.

"Why not?" I asked. "She was obviously giving you a long look."

That is simply not possible. Now Blodwen was getting involved.

"A vampire would never consort willingly with a goblin," Nose Wart explained, his expression remarkably serious and thoughtful. "They are a powerful being and we are...soldiers."

"Fodder!" I snapped. "Most of the Supernatural community seems to regard you as little more than fodder to be thrown at an enemy with no regard to your lives."

"That is the way of this world," Nose Wart said with a shrug.

I don't know what had me more steamed at the moment: the fact that I'd been little better in my regard for the goblin; or that there were such insane and antiquated ideas of where love can sprout. I would think that beings that have been around for centuries might be a bit more enlightened. Hadn't these people heard of *Romeo & Juliet*? The Hatfields and the McCoys? Amber Tamblen and David Cross? Okay, that last one is probably the closest thing to a Nose Wart and Devonna pairing.

"Miss Birch?" Nancy called down. "Is it...acceptable for us to return to the basement?"

"Sure," I called back as I willed Sharkmouth away.

The three vampires returned, but this time they had a fourth person in tow. This was a human, of that there could be no doubt. Humans are all dying a little bit each day, and that makes all of you smell appetizing to a ghoul; not to the point where I would randomly start attacking you and going on a binge, but you do smell good. The closer to death you are, the better you smell. Don't get me started on what it is like to walk (or even drive) past a senior citizen community.

"Ava, I'm Brandy McKeon. I'm the one who called you."

I looked at this woman and tried to picture her smashing into other women while rocketing along on roller skates. I think I may have mentioned that I had a slight recollection of roller derby from back in the 80s. Mostly I remember all the blonde-haired beauties with the Los Angeles T-Birds and their arch enemy, Mizz Georgia Hase, (emphasis on the MIZZ part and that last name sounding like the chubby Cartwright from Bonanza).

Her spiked blonde hair was dyed a pretty shade of lavender. Her green eyes were bright and looked like she had a million and one dirty secrets that she couldn't wait to whisper in your ear; although there was a shade of purple under those eyes from what looked like a mostly healed broken nose. She also had a split upper lip, but none of it detracted from her girl-next-door prettiness.

"Wow," Brandy gasped when I turned to give her my full gaze. Since I was in the basement of a vampire's house, I had not bothered to get any of my stuff out of my bag; things like the dark glasses that hid the solid black orbs that are my eyes, or any of the air brush make-up to make my gray skin a more human shade of tan or whitish-pink. "Nobody told me that you looked like..." She sort of stopped speaking and just stood with her mouth open and a bright red blush in her cheeks.

Jiminy crackers, that reaction was becoming pretty common in this little basement, I thought.

"Like a ghoul?" Nose Wart offered.

The woman looked around and began to rub her arms like she had a chill. Her gaze passed right over the little goblin at least three times, but never lingered more than a second.

Humans can't see the goblin, Blodwen reminded me.

Lisa can see him, I countered.

She is has a minimal amount of psychic ability, and now she is a Templar. They are fitted with special contacts that allow them to see into a deeper spectrum.

I guess I'd simply forgotten about the whole 'humans can't see goblins' thing for the moment. Up until today, I guess I hadn't actually been in the company of a true, living human since I'd entered this world of the supernatural. (No, that isn't a mistake; I didn't capitalize the word 'supernatural' in this case because I am not referring to our race...or are we a species? Hmm, that is something I never pondered.)

"Is there a problem?" I asked simply, snapping Brandy's attention back to me.

"I just got a weird case of the heebie-jeebies," she muttered like she was doing a little daydreaming of her own. Her voice had that absent quality like when you respond out of habit rather than truly responding to the person you are speaking to at that moment. Sort of like when your boyfriend says, "Sure, babe!" while he is watching the playoffs and you ask him if he wants to go antiquing in ten minutes.

"So, what did you expect me to look like?" I asked, honestly curious.

"Umm…" Again the woman seemed to just hang up mentally in mid-sentence. She blinked her eyes and shook her head and then looked me in the eyes. "I never gave it any thought. I mean, vampires look normal until they show a little fang."

"So you just figured I would look like a human." It wasn't a question. When she nodded, I did something that I'm not entirely proud of. Yeah, you probably guessed it. I let the switchdigits pop and then brought on Sharkmouth. "Surprise!" I said with just a little growl.

I thought she might scream or something. I had no idea that she was going to scream, wet her pants, and then faint; in that order.

"I didn't see that coming," I said with a weak laugh and a shrug.

As the vampires scrambled to tend to the fallen woman, I went and grabbed my gear so that I could at least look partially human when Brandy woke up. Nose Wart was a real trooper and helped me spray paint my hands. I decided that I would give myself the "Farmer's Tan" edition of a paint job since I wasn't planning on letting anybody see me naked any time soon.

***

"I'm so sorry," Brandy gasped for the fourth or fifth time as Tish and Devonna hovered over her, each holding ice packs and cold rags that they had used on the woman to help bring her around. "I just did not expect—"

"A monster," I finished for her. I heard the tone of my voice and quickly changed it since I was sort of sounding a little like a bitch. Oh, and just a note fellas…it is okay for us to claim that status, it is never okay for you to wield that word against us. Sort of like another word, not nearly as serious, but trust me when I tell you that it is a sure fire way to escalate any argument to a nuclear attack in a single syllable. "I have not been around many humans since becoming a ghoul," I admitted, trying to sound contrite.

"Is it against the rules to ask you how you become a ghoul? I mean, did another ghoul bite you, or did you eat some exotic plant?" Brandy sat up and accepted the ice pack from Tish, slapping it on the back of her neck like a pro.

"Suicide," I began. I saw her eyes go wide as I told her a very condensed version of my "transformation" into the ghoul I am today.

"And you say that there is a goblin in this room with us right now?" Brandy looked around, squinting as if that would help her see better.

I glanced at Nose Wart who had moved over to the woman and was sniffing around her, cocking his head from side to side every few seconds, making it very difficult not to make the comparison between him and a puppy. At this exact moment, he looked like he was about to lick her elbow!

"Nose Wart!" I hissed. "Get over here."

The little goblin started and then scurried to my side. "She smells of battle, Just Ava. She has damage."

I looked down at the goblin and pursed my lips. "What do you mean?"

"Inside," he whispered. "There is bleeding."

"Have you seen a doctor?" I looked up at the woman who was regarding me like you might if you passed a vagrant on the street that was engrossed in an argument with his shopping cart.

"What? Why?" Brandy said, still searching for something she could not see.

"Nose Wart says that you are bleeding inside."

Private Eyes

"That was good work, Nose Wart," I told the goblin as I sat in the van parked in front of the hospital.

I'd just received a text from Nancy that reported the doctors had discovered a small rupture of the spleen. She was being prepped for surgery at this exact moment.

Two of Brandy's roller derby team mates were on the way to the hospital and would pick me up. They would be driving an old Taurus station wagon which should make them easy to spot since there aren't too many of those on the road any more. The vampire assured me that I would be safe going with them, and that they would be taking me to the old exposition center that now acted as the local roller derby rink.

"It is secure enough for a vampire to stay in, so I assume it will be okay for you if it gets too close to dawn and you have to shelter in place," Nancy had said cheerfully like she was sharing a cake recipe with me or something.

I wanted to ask her for more details, but she'd already hung up. Now I sat with Nose Wart, waiting for a burgundy Ford Taurus wagon to pull in.

"So, I had no idea that you could smell injuries like that," I said with true appreciation. "You might have saved that woman's life."

Nose Wart shrugged as if it were no big deal. "Smell is our strongest sense."

"Sort of like those cats that stroll around senior centers and curl up on the lap of the person who has cancer." I knew I was probably botching that analogy, but I knew there were always kicker stories like that on the local news every few months when they ran out of other useless crap to over-report on.

A set of headlights cut off whatever response Nose Wart was going to give. I saw a very ratty station wagon sputter into the lot, smoke belching from the tail pipe. And while the original color might have once been burgundy, this car had more Bondo and gray primer paint than anything else.

The car pulled up right next to us and two women emerged. One of them was way taller than six feet and looked like she might have genetic ties to my jötunn except for the fact that her hair was a dark brown shade. Her nose, what was left of it, sat almost sideways on her face and had obviously been busted a few more times than it had been set. She had lips so thin that they were almost invisible. Her muscled forearms were heavily tattooed with a strikingly beautiful series of vines and roses that seemed to contradict the gruff demeanor that this woman exuded with her hard glare and twisted scowl.

The other woman was as opposite as any woman could be from her cohort. She was a petite little thing that looked like one of those tiny gymnasts from the Chinese Olympic team. Her black hair was pulled back in a ponytail that really helped accent the delicate slant of her eyes.

"Ava?" the tiny woman said. "Miss Ava Birch, we're here to collect y'all and take ya to the arena."

I don't care who you are or how liberated you think your mind is, but when you hear somebody of Asian heritage speaking with a heavy Texas accent…it's pretty damn funny.

I climbed out of the van, Nose Wart close on my heels. "That would be me." I gave a little wave and tried to flash a smile, but the scowl I was getting from the human mountain of female meat was not all that welcoming, and the smile quickly died on my lips.

The tiny woman shot a look over her shoulder at her companion and it was like somebody hit a light switch. The glare and scowl vanished in an instant. It wasn't replaced by what I would call a smile, but at least it was not outwardly hostile in appearance.

"Sorry, but nobody gave me any names," I said as I closed the van door and walked to the waiting station wagon.

"They call me Claire Lee Insane, and this is Rock Star Hell." The feminine mountain turned and hiked a thumb over her shoulder at the name on the back of her Jersey. It read: Rock*Hell.

"I was thinking something like Queen Kong," I muttered.

"Oh, that name is sort of sacred," Claire Lee Insane replied with a smile. "That is one of the Old School Hall of Famers. Nobody on wheels would dare use her name."

I seemed to recall a rather large and unpleasant woman that went by that moniker, but I'd thought she was a pro wrassler. I shrugged and made my way to the open back door, sliding into what was left of a back seat that was more pokey springs than padding.

We did not have far to drive, and the road we were on was lined with what looked like old abandoned warehouses. Basically not the best part of town, and I was a little surprised when we pulled into a parking lot and I saw about a hundred women of all shapes and sizes gathered in groups or heading into one long, building with flaking green paint and a metal roof. A huge sign hung over the two sets of wide open double-doors. The sign declared: Roller Queens Jamboree! TONIGHT!

I emerged from the car and had to dial back my hearing. There was a multitude of conversations taking place, but the mood was universal. These women were apprehensive at best, and some were downright scared. Still there was also a sense of excitement.

As we parked in the dimly lit lot, a pack of about twenty women broke away from the gathering and headed our way. Before the car was even shut off and still going through its chugging and coughing as it tried in vain to remain running, we were surrounded.

"These are our girls," Claire Lee, said over her shoulder as she popped her door open and climbed out to greet the throng.

I reached for my own door, but a meaty hand had reached back and grabbed my arm. I froze, but not out of fear. At least that is what I kept telling myself as I slowly turned my head to regard the woman known to me only as Rock*Hell. I glanced down at her hand, and then let my gaze travel up to meet hers.

"I'll be watching you, ghoul. You make so much as a twitch that I don't like and we are gonna have problems." Her glare didn't show any reaction when I let my fingers go into switch mode.

That is when it hit me! The craziness of everything up to this point, coupled with not really being alert to anything had caused me to miss something that was very important. I saw the outline under the black glove covering the hand that held my wrist.

"A Templar?" I scoffed.

Instantly, Nose Wart went for the blade at his hip, but just as fast, the woman let go of me and struck the goblin with a back-hand that sent him slamming into the driver's side back seat door. His body went limp, and I did a quick sniff to confirm that he was not dead.

"You ever touch him again, and I don't care where we are or what you think that ring on your finger will do to help, but I promise that I will shred you like cheese and hang that little piece of jewelry around my neck as a trophy and a warning to any other Templar that thinks he or she really wants a piece of me."

It was brief, and maybe I imagined it because it is what I was hoping for, but I swear I saw just a crinkle of what I was going to call fear as it tugged at the corners of the large woman's eyes. I opened my door and emerged into the throng of jacked up estrogen. These women were all sporting an assortment of bruises and a few wore splints or braces.

"Can I assume that you ladies faced this team of Valkyries?" I said by way of greeting.

There were several nods along with some creative curses that Nose Wart would be proud of if he'd been conscious to hear them. I shot a glance back at the car as Rock*Hell emerged, making sure that she did not do any further damage to my little friend.

Friend.

That word echoed in my mind. It was a stunning revelation when it made itself known to my little brain. Nose Wart was my friend. I had no idea when that had happened, but I knew it was true the moment that word popped into my head.

"Speak of the devils," one of the women snarled as a trio of ice blue RVs pulled in and rumbled to a stop.

I could not help myself and found that I was wandering towards the three luxury vehicles that probably cost more apiece than all these women made in a year combined. I was about twenty yards away when the strains of *Die Walküre* began to blare from the lead bus.

As if on cue, all three RVs had their side doors open and out came a team of blonde-haired, blue-eyed women who all looked exactly how you would expect a Valkyrie to look. They all had long braids on each side of their round heads; each wore metal breastplates, and had some sort of leather thing that looked like a one-piece bathing suit under it. To finish the look, each wore a flowing fur cape that I am pretty certain would piss off most of those PETA folks since it was obviously real and looked like it might be made from a polar bear.

My goodness, Blodwen exclaimed from inside my head. *I have not seen a Valkyrie for centuries.*

I watched the Valkyries move for the entrance of the building and it was not lost on me that all the women who had been gathered in front of the skating arena and been in the midst of various conversations had all gone silent. Everybody was watching these warriors as they crossed the open parking lot; and there was no denying it; these ladies were combatants.

So why are they here in Texas, and why are they involved in Roller Derby? I mused inwardly.

I was standing there with that single thought swirling in my head when I felt something stir in my mind. More specifically, the area where the current residents were housed. To be exact…it was Mystify.

Let him out, Ava! Blodwen seemed to shout. I could detect something in her voice that was very close to urgency.

I paused for a moment, worried that I might not be able to seal him away again. The last thing I needed was his presence bouncing around in my head; especially since I would be returning to his former residence later on during this little trip to take out Claude. I still did not know if these two were in cahoots with each other. I still believed that I'd been duped just a little when I'd been lured to Dallas not too long ago.

I will deal with him and help you seal him away if it is a problem, Blodwen promised.

With a sigh, I let Mystify out of his mental prison cell, but I was very wary, and already had preparations to secure him away again if he got out of line.

An elf! Mystify said with obvious awe. *And not just any elf, but one of power that has a royal bloodline.*

A what? I started to unleash a barrage of questions when I felt something tickle in the back of my brain.

I turned to my left and it was as if my body was some sort of elven divining rod. I could feel the presence of this creature despite not having any earthly idea of what I was looking for. All I could think of was Liv Tyler from the *Lord of the Rings* trilogy.

When my eyes came to rest on her, I actually slapped my forehead. She was beautiful, her features delicate. She had hair that was emerald green and something told me it wasn't a dye job. Her eyes sparkled with an unnaturally bright blue that almost seemed to glow in the poorly lit near darkness of the parking lot. She had an adorable button nose and ruby red lips that I, once again, did not believe to be enhanced by anything.

Despite my staring, she did not seem to notice me, but I could feel her presence like a physical thing and had the urge to approach her.

That is a Psychic reaction, Mystify said. *Obviously you are developing one of my powers. A Psychic can feel an uninvited Supernatural that enters his or her territory. We can track them down and that internal sense is what makes it impossible for an outsider to enter our district. With time and practice, you can even discern the type.*

I taste...grass, I said inwardly.

Then you now know what an elf feels like.

Wait, if this is the case, then why am I not getting anything from the Valkyries? I asked as I watched the female elf follow what I had to assume was her roller derby team into the arena.

It can mean that you have not fully absorbed my power, or... Mystify went quiet and I waited patiently to see if he would continue, or if maybe he was up to something. Yeah, I have serious trust issues. *Perhaps the Valkyries are here at Claude's request.*

"Ava!" a voice called from behind me.

I turned to see Claire Lee and the other girls coming my way. I also noticed that Nose Wart had regained his senses and was following the group, making it a point to cut directly in front of Rock*Hell as he spotted me and hurried to my side.

"You will get to see those brutes in action in just a few minutes. The first match will be The Valkyries versus The Hellbound Foxes," Claire said with just a hint of excitement. "Two of the Foxes have vowed to take down the Valkyrie known as Hildegard. She is the one most of us agree to be the enforcer of The Valkyries. Granted, all of them play rough, but Hildegard looks like she is really trying to damage people. So far, there have been a dozen league protests filed against just her and we are only two weeks into the season." I walked beside Claire Lee as she gave me the lowdown and found that I was becoming less distracted by her twang now that I'd heard it for a while.

When we entered the building, I was amazed to discover that both sides of the large oval track had numerous sections of bleachers set along the walls that were packed with men, women, and even children. There were booths with merchandise and concessions scattered about, and the atmosphere was amazingly festive. I wondered if this was what it was like at the Colosseum in Rome during its glory days.

"So is this what it is like every night you gals skate?" I asked.

"We wish!" Claire Lee said with obvious longing in her voice. "This is one of our big jamborees. All the teams skate tonight in shorter matches. The pairings were done by random draw."

"Sure glad the Foxes drew The Valkyries," one of the women sighed with obvious relief. As she passed me and took a seat on a long bench with the rest of her team, I was able to read the name on the back of her jersey. It fit the woman rather nicely.

The name was 'Cleosmacktra' and she had very straight, jet black hair. Her skin was a mocha shade that made the blue contacts she was wearing really pop. She had the Liz Taylor make-up thing going around the eyes in pale blues and greens with the heavy black eye-liner, and her lips were painted a blood red that would give a vampire the munchies.

As I stood taking in the circus-like atmosphere, I had a chance to let my eyes wander down the line of gals who were all in the act of lacing up their skates. I now understood why the names on the jerseys of The Valkyries had raised such red flags with Brandy—VaVa Vroom, Smash Effect, Angel A Mercy, Bad JuJu, Rita Haywire, and my personal favorite, Shirley Temper declared the entertaining aliases these women used on the track.

I could tell that they were getting their game faces on...or whatever it is that sports people do before taking the field...er...rink? I was just going to be in the way, so I decided to wander around alone and take in more of the festivities.

Also, that would now give me a chance to check out The Valkyries a bit closer, as well as that elf. Since I could still feel that inner divining rod thingy working inside me, I decided to check the elf out first. I was surrounded by a lot of people, so I decided to kneel and pretend like I was tying my shoe in order to give Nose Wart a little mission of his own on the sly.

"I want you to keep an eye on the Templar for me. See if she is somebody that we have to be concerned with. I don't like

68

having my focus on something else and end up giving that be-hemoth the chance to get the drop on me."

"Yes, Just Ava!" Nose Wart gave a low bow and scampered off through the forest of legs to do my bidding.

Knowing that he was watching my back made me feel a whole lot safer. *He would be proud and honored if you told him that*, Butt Pimple coaxed.

I was sort of impressed at how she was still watching out for her man even in death. It was just another thing that made me realize that I'd been taking my goblin friends for granted. That was going to come to a halt for sure.

I continued to stroll casually through the crowd, occasional-ly catching a whiff of somebody who might not yet realize just how close to death they were. One woman in particular made me stop and do a double-take. If my eyes had been shut, I would have thought her to be dead. I wished for just an instant that I knew what was wrong like when Nose Wart had told me about Brandy and her internal bleeding. It might be something like a detectable cancer that could be cut out, giving her a chance at a longer life. As it was (or smelled), I didn't see the woman lasting the week.

At last I discovered my target. It was only a little surprising to discover that she was part of The Hellbound Foxes squad. They were all in a circle—the Foxes, I mean—and had arms over each other's shoulders doing that thing where they sway back and forth. One of the women was chanting something about "Who's tough?" to which the rest of the team would shout, "Foxes!" "What we doin' to them Valkyries?" "Sending them to Hell!"

I stayed back as the ritual continued, but my eyes did drift away from the elven woman long enough to seek out the little band of Valkyries. They were not involved in any of the pre-game ritual stuff that the Foxes were into at the moment. They were simply cinching up their gear and occasionally beating themselves and their team mates on the chest, helmet, and shoulders with loud and thunderous smacks that made me cringe at the thought of any of those women hitting me like that for any reason.

Now that I saw them in full regalia, it was not a stretch to think of these women as actual Valkyries. Of course, I knew that normal humans would have no such thoughts. That sort of stuff simply did not exist in the mortal world. These were just really gorgeous women with amazingly fit bodies decked out in shining armor that the observer would mistakenly dismiss as fake.

This was the real deal; and so were these women. I watched one in particular as she pulled her winged helmet on and cinched it under the chin. The others had similar helms, but some were sporting horns instead of wings. The woman I watched seemed to freeze for a moment, and then her head popped up and her eyes went straight to me and bored into me.

I was initially surprised that she honed in and locked on so fast. But it was what she did next that made me trip over my own two feet and almost end up on my face, She smiled big and then brought up her left hand with the index finger pointing directly at me; then she very slowly and deliberately brought her right hand over, the index finger making a slow deliberate scrape across the index finger of the left hand. She "tsk'd" me!

I was in the middle of an internal debate about the prudence of just strolling up to this woman when a pack of women on skates rolled past. They were en route to the oval skating surface.

I guess I will get to see what this is all about, I mused as I headed for the bleachers where I could get a good look at the action.

The Hellbound Foxes were moving toward the gate that swung open and granted them access to the skating area. I smirked at the name on the elven gal's jersey; Not-So-Hairy-Kari. Then it hit me like a shotgun blast to the chest! I was willing to bet that this was Morgan's pal. This was the one who I was supposed to secure the Dallas Psychic job for while I was here dealing with the Valkyrie problem.

I had to wonder if perhaps Morgan was aware of how these two jobs now seemed to be intertwined with one another. She couldn't know that Claude had brought in Valkyries…could

70

she? Hmm…it wouldn't be the first time that she sent me into a job blind. In fact, that was more of a standard procedure than sending me in with any actual knowledge.

A roar from the crowd snapped me back to the situation at hand. It seemed that The Valkyries were now coming onto the track. I was once again taken back to the professional wrestling glory days of the mid-to-late 80s. The Four Horsemen led by The Nature Boy, Ric Flair, were the evil villains of that era. And, male or female, redneck or Wall Street executive, if you don't know who The Nature Boy, Ric Flair is…you have my pity.

The people in the stands were an equal mix of those who booed and hollered some rather derogatory remarks, and those who cheered wildly. One man made the mistake of letting his love or hate for The Valkyries take him from his seat to the wide aisle that the women were skating down as they approached the entry gate (it happened so fast that I couldn't tell which side he fell on in that regard).

He jumped in front of the trio of women leading the procession and the Valkyrie in the center punched him so fast that it was a blur even to my eyes. That single punch sent the man flying up and backwards a good dozen feet. He crashed into three other eager roller derby fans who all promptly tossed the man aside where he landed on the concrete floor that already showed signs of being sticky from spilled beverages and such.

I winced. Whether it was from witnessing the punch the man sustained, or at the idea of being face down on this floor that was only second in "grody to the max" factor to a porn theater, I could not be absolutely certain. But then I caught a whiff of something in the general direction of the body that was not showing any signs of movement.

Surely these Valkyries would not actually kill somebody in this very public setting.

That was the thought blossoming in my mind up until the Valkyrie that I'd made that brief but direct eye contact with a few moments ago gave me a little wave and then winked. The smell was growing stronger and yummier by the second and I altered my course to take me to where that man still lay on the ground almost completely ignored by the fans that were now becoming more vocal and boisterous by the second.

"Grab that body and get it back behind the concession carts," a voice said to me in a lilting and seductive tone that made me once again ask myself if perhaps I shouldn't take Katy Perry's advice and just kiss a girl to see if I like it.

My gaze swept the area and I was amazed when I found Not-So-Hairy-Kari looking directly at me as she skated past from the track with the rest of the Foxes. Her lips moved, and that voice came again.

"I don't like it either, but we can't let this place erupt in a panic." The elven vixen gave me a slight nod and I could see her lips barely moving as she basically did little more than mouth the words I was hearing.

I was struck by a very strange inspiration as I arrived at the man's side. I rolled him over and instantly recognized the glassy-eyed stare of death.

"C'mon, Jack!" I said in as cajoling a tone as I could manage while I slipped my arm under and around the fresh corpse.

I had to sort of swallow back Sharkmouth as I hauled the man to his feet and made like *Weekend at Bernie's* as I basically carried him to the concession carts. Humans are funny. They see what they want to see and have the ability to ignore something that is staring them in the face if it does not fit into their perception of the world. That is the only explanation that I have for why people just flowed around us as they hurried to their seats and we made like spawning salmon and worked our way against the current until we were at last behind a little trailer with the words "Elephant Ears Here!" in bright blue against the white background of its cracked vinyl siding.

With one final look over my shoulder to ensure that we were not being observed, I gobbled the man up as fast as I could. It had been a while since I'd eaten a corpse that was still dressed and was already dreading the fact that I would regurgitate the clothing after I'd finished eating. I was just about to the legs when I heard a roar from the crowd that came right on the heels of a collective "ooooooo" that let me know somebody must've just gotten blasted on the track.

I wolfed down the last few bites and was in mid-gurge when Nose Wart sprinted up to me panting and sounding like his lungs wanted to turn inside out.

"I told you to keep an eye on that Templar. I need to know you are watching my back here, Nose Wart," I scolded.

"That...is the...problem..." he managed between heaving gasps as he tried to get his air back. "The Templar is under attack!"

That Ghoul Ava on a Roll!

7

Come on, Eileen

"Say what!" I barked, motioning for him to lead the way. "Who or what is attacking the Templar?"

"A pair of revenants," was Nose Wart's reply. He was still a bit winded, but at least he could talk without having to gasp for breath in between each word.

I followed him and had to really force myself to not look back towards the track when another massive crash sounded, bringing another collective groan from the crowd. *What the hell was I missing back there!*

"What would bring revenants to someplace like this?" I grumbled aloud, but basically to myself as I hurried along on Nose Wart's heels.

"There has to be a vamp nearby," Nose Wart called over his shoulder. "All revenants serve a master."

Hmm, learn something new every day.

I rounded a corner that revealed a long, narrow corridor that ended in a pair of double doors with red exit signs hanging above them. Super ghoul hearing or not, the sounds of a scuffle were obvious. I took off at a sprint and heard Nose Wart give a little yelp of surprise as I sped away from him.

In two huge loping bounds, I was at the doors and threw one open with a loud bang of metal slamming into concrete. I winced a little as I saw the door rip free from its top hinge.

Rock*Hell shot a quick glance over her shoulder and her look was one that wanted to be relief, but considering our brief and less-than-sociable relationship status, it was clear that she was a teensy bit concerned that I might be here to give assistance to the pair of fanged and feral creatures that were hissing and snarling at her under the dim glow of the flickering loading dock light that stood sentinel over the scene.

"Looks like you could use a hand," I said, giving a nod to the large woman who had blood dripping down her left arm from a nasty rip at the top of her shoulder.

"I wouldn't refuse it," the woman said, caution still ringing in her voice.

I stepped into the deserted loading area and let the switch digits come. Nose Wart exploded through the door a second later and had his rusty little blade in hand in a flash.

"Which one are we killing?" he asked.

I knew what he meant, but I wasn't sure if the Templar knew she was included in that question. I gave a nod to the female revenant with the mane of crazy dark hair that looked like it belonged on a Rastafarian lion more so than a human. Nose Wart didn't need any further clarification. With a howl that was a lot like what a Bassett Hound might do when a fire truck rumbles past with its siren blaring, the little goblin warrior charged in.

I have no idea where he produced it from, but in a flash, his little rusty sword was replaced by what might have once been an ornate chair leg that had been sharpened to a point. Since I was without my arsenal of stakes and squirt guns filled with holy water, my goal was to simply lop off the head of the fanged menace. Even if it remained…umm…well, I guess 'alive' is gonna have to suffice until I can think of another way to describe an undead creature that is not technically living but still very functional and—

I took a shoulder to my gut as the male revenant decided that I was either a tastier target or less scary looking that the she-hulk Templar that seemed to have grown a few more inches and packed on another fifty pounds of muscle now that I was seeing her up close and in combat action. Truth be told, I would have attacked me too if given the choice between us. Even in full-on ghoul mode, I am nowhere near as scary looking as Rock*Hell.

I staggered back, but fortunately I did not lose my footing and was able to bring a forearm up to block the male vamp from getting those gnashing teeth anywhere near my throat. He apparently did not have any problem redirecting his bite, and chomping down on my forearm.

I'd never been bitten by a vamp before. It was creepy. I could actually feel something tug at my...essence? It was as if whatever made me Ava was being siphoned away. However, the feeling was very brief. Describing it actually took several seconds longer than the actual sensation. In a flash, the male revenant jerked back and began to spit like Gordon Ramsey might after a bite of my cooking. Only, the spit was sending up tendrils of a very funky smoke.

Ghoul blood is rumored to be toxic to a vamp, as would the blood of any undead creature. Vampires need the power of life blood, I heard Blodwen sort of lecturing in the background as the male threw himself on his back and began to thrash about wildly and with such speed that he was becoming a blur. It sort of reminded me of that creepy effect in horror movies where the head thrashes about when a possessed person is transforming. Only, this was the entire body of the revenant moving at a million miles an hour back and forth in a space of only a few inches in either direction. Like I said...creepy.

I was not about to touch the thing while it did all that vibrating and thrashing, so I spun to see how Nose Wart was faring. I was impressed. He had positioned himself between Rock*Hell and the female revenant. The Templar did not have a stake or anything that would serve to drive through the vamp's heart, so she was basically fighting a losing battle if we had not arrived on the scene. Provided we all survived this little encounter, that was a fact I would not be letting her forget.

The female vamp was down in a crouch, and, since she was naked, it was easy to see her muscles tense as she prepared to spring. Apparently Nose Wart's eyes were as good as mine. He ducked as the revenant came flying. At the last possible second he drove the spike up and buried it between the revenants breasts. She exploded like a bag of flour. The coarse grit showered both my goblin friend and the Templar. I noticed right away that it wasn't sparkly like when I'd seen other vampires bite the dust (no pun intended).

The noise behind me jerked me around and I was prepared to fend off the male. However, what I was greeted by was the body going all black like charcoal for a handful of seconds and then it crumbled into a dark smear on the asphalt.

The sound of hands clapping came from above and I looked up in time to see a pair of red, glowing eyes regarding me from inside a hoody that was pulled in tight to the point that it reminded me of Kenny from *South Park* before they vanished in less than a blink of an eye. I would not be able to identify the assailant or master or whatever the hell that vampire was, but I did know for certain that he or she was a vamp. My super sniffer never fails me when it comes to that sort of thing. To put it bluntly, vampires smell gross.

"So, Race is right about you," the big woman said with a wince as she examined the rip on her arm.

"Huh?" That's me at my elegant best.

"He said that the offshoot faction of Templars has it all wrong and that you are nothing like the old legends. He has been telling anybody who will listen that we need to band together and support you. He thinks you are important for the battle that has been brewing for decades…hell…maybe even centuries considering the fact that Templars and Supernaturals are like slow cookers and can often take years plotting out the simplest move just because they have the time and want to cover all the bases."

"Uh-huh." *Words, Ava, use your words!* I goaded myself. "So, Race has been talking about me."

I think I heard Blodwen slap her forehead. I was making a really strong case for the people who wanted me dead simply by acting like such a dork. I took a mental breath and then tried again.

"He thinks I am going to be part of some big war thingy?" Okay. The word 'thingy' was probably not the best choice, but I felt like I was on the way to better representing myself.

"Race Mitchell believes that you may very well be the key to returning order," the woman said with no hint of being nasty or even the teensiest bit sarcastic.

"Look, I don't want to be a problem for you or anybody else," I started slowly, but felt just a smidge of confidence beginning to grow as the large woman regarded me with more interest and less disdain than when we'd first met. "I never asked for this. And nobody has really filled me in on the finer points of what being a ghoul is supposed to mean. Oh, sure, I keep being told a number of things, but many of them conflict with what somebody else says and it has gotten to the point that I honestly have no idea what to do…much less who to trust. I'm sure that both sides see the other as evil…that's usually the way of things in a war. And I would feel awful if I threw in with the real villains and helped defeat the good guys in this simply because I don't know which side is right…or…good? Is either side good in this little thing?"

The woman stared at me for much longer than was comfortable and then a smile began to crease her face until it was a huge grin. She reached over and slapped me on the shoulder in what I was pretty sure was meant to be a sign of camaraderie, but if I'd been a normal human, I probably would have had a bruise that was just about be the size of one of her gigantic hands.

"So, is your name really Ava?" the woman asked as she headed for the door that led back inside the building.

"Yeah, why wouldn't it be?" That seemed like an odd question—hers, not mine.

"Most Supernaturals change their names after they leave their human side behind," Rock*Hell explained.

"Yeah, well, for what it's worth, I get told quite often that I still think way too much like a human." I gave a slight shrug as I walked through the door. "I imagine your parents didn't give you the name you wear on that jersey."

The woman laughed, and it was actually a very pleasant

sound. She sighed and looked around as if to be sure we were alone; which, except for her, me, and Nose Wart, we were.

"Eileen Jakovich." The woman extended a hand to me and it actually took me a few seconds to realize that she was offering to shake hands.

"Well, Eileen, I guess we better get back to the others before they start to miss us."

"Just do me a favor." The woman stopped and fixed me with a very serious gaze that would have probably unnerved me if she and I were still on each other's shit list.

"Sure," I agreed with a shrug.

"Nobody calls me Eileen."

"What do they call you?"

"Usually just Rock or bitch."

There was a pause, and then she smiled again which quickly morphed into laughter. I sure hoped that things remained as they were right this moment between me and Eileen. She was actually a pretty groovy lady.

Yeah, I said groovy. Personally, I think people should resume firing that word off a bit more often.

"Rock it is," I said as we turned and took off up the hallway at a trot to the rumble of a crowd that sounded like they were in quite a frenzy.

Nose Wart actually took off at a faster run and reached the corner well ahead of us. Even from back here, I could see his head tilt from one side to the other. The only thing that I couldn't tell was if it was due to interest, confusion, or excitement.

I finally reached the corner and had to skid to a halt to avoid slamming into a family of four that were making a hurried exit. The father had his hands on the shoulder of the little girl and was making his own body into a bit of a shield to keep her from looking back and glimpsing whatever was going on on the track. The mother had the boy by the hand and was going to dislocate the shoulder if she jerked much harder.

What I saw when I finally slipped past the family that was now starting to be joined by a few other clusters making for the nearest exit was a blood bath. Seriously, that is the best way to describe it.

The Foxes were scattered around the ring, each of them being pummeled mercilessly by a Valkyrie. I saw no sign of any refs or anybody that might be inclined to put an end to the melee.

"C'mon, Eileen," I urged as I took off at a sprint for the entrance to the skating area.

The large oval track was painted black, so it hid a lot of the evidence, but the light blue walls were splattered with the red life fluid in senseless patterns that marked some of the worst of the violence.

The one thing that instantly jumped out at me was the missing elf. She'd either run for it, been captured, or was skulking through this crowd; one thing for sure, she was not in the skating area taking a beating with her team.

"Typical Psychic," I muttered.

"Huh?" Eileen was beside me now and also surveying the damage.

"Nothing." While we might be making progress towards an amicable relationship, I wasn't about to trust her with anything that I deemed serious.

I watched as one of the Foxes tried to climb over the barricade, only to be pulled back, spun around, and punched square in the face. Again I examined the crowd. The ones remaining were eating this up.

"Isn't anybody gonna try and stop this?" I spun around, facing a group of trucker hat-wearing yay-hoos sitting on the nearest set of bleachers.

"C'mon, sweetheart," one of the men tried to pacify me, "this ain't nothin' but pro wrasslin' on skates. This stuff is as fake as a centerfold's boobies."

"Idiot," I snarled, pointing to the carnage just a few feet away. "Those women are being beaten to death right in front of your eyes!"

The man gave me a dismissive wave, his attention already returning to the track where the Foxes were now mostly sprawled on the floor; each of them now straddled by a Valkyrie that continued to rain down blows without mercy. I looked around and saw that families with children were not the only people slinking out of the arena. Several of the other teams were making slow progress towards the exits as well.

The only team that currently showed no signs of leaving was the Hot-n-Steamy Rollers. They were all clustered around Claire Lee. I could tell from here that they were in the middle of a very spirited debate. A hunch told me that they were about to do something very stupid.

I didn't have to wait long to have that assumption confirmed. As one, they all let loose with a yell that was just a bit too screechy to be an actual war cry, but I gave them points for trying.

"Ohh…" I started.

"…crap," Eileen finished for me.

We shot each other a knowing look and made for the gate that opened to the track. I was only having one little problem. The closer that I got to the mayhem, the more the smells started to tickle my belly. I didn't need Nose Wart's super power ability to know that a few of these gals might not make it out of here alive.

A renewed cascade of cheers sounded as the Hot-n-Steamy Rollers rumbled onto the track. At least they had a smart game plan by the looks of things. Instead of going one-on-one with any of the Valkyries, they were swarming just the few closest with four-against-one odds.

Eileen and I reached the gate just behind Nose Wart, and I pointed to one of the Valkyries that was close as well as having her back to us. We made for her, Eileen on skates and me on foot which only made our already huge size difference that much greater. Lucky for me, I have some enhanced abilities and had no problem keeping up with the enormous missile that was Rock*Hell as she hurtled herself at the back of the Valkyrie.

The collision was a meaty slap, and the crowd erupted in cheers and even a few boos as we pounced on the Valkyrie. I sprung the last several feet, careful to try and not do anything too crazy lest the spectators see something that they couldn't reconcile.

The Valkyrie instantly let go of the inert and unconscious body of the woman she'd been beating on, spinning to face us. She went from being on her knees to standing in a blur that I knew had to be unnatural.

"Jesus," Eileen gasped, actually staggering back a step from the Valkyrie who had a good three or four inches on her.

If she had Eileen in height, she absolutely towered over me. I was admittedly a bit intimidated. After all, this was a creature that I had no actual knowledge of when it came to strengths or weaknesses. It was in that second that I realized how much intel I'd actually received from Morgan on my past jobs. It had always been one of my gripes, but suddenly those teeny nuggets seemed to be a helluva lot more.

"What do we have here?" the Valkyrie said with a snort.

"Ava Birch. I'm the ghoul sent here to run you out of town."

The Valkyrie's eyes flashed over to me, and that was when I realized that she had not been referring to me. She was fixed on Eileen, measuring her up with what looked like a trace of approval.

"You might make a good Sister of the Shield," the woman rumbled, her eyes and Eileen's locked on each other as they started to move in a slight counter-clockwise direction.

"And those braids of yours might look good hanging from my car's radio antennae." Eileen clenched her fists.

"Umm, excuse me," I interjected. I wasn't too surprised when neither woman broke eye contact to look my direction. "I am only going to ask you this one time...gather your stuff and leave. Go back to whomever hired you and tell that person you quit."

It was like in those movies where one person is trying to talk over the noise to the guy or gal they are with, and just as they talk at full volume, the crowd goes silent and everybody turns and looks. I swear I heard my voice echo in the massive warehouse that acted as the arena for this little derby tournament.

"And who might you be?" At least the Valkyrie seemed to notice that I was present.

I glanced around and saw several of the other Valkyries heading our direction. The few that had been jumped by Eileen's team mates were shrugging aside their attackers like it was nothing and coming to gather around the three of us.

"My name is Ava Birch and I—" the rest of my declaration was cut off by the crowd erupting into a chant.

"Fight...fight...fight..."

I looked around and was not surprised to see the yay-hoos leading the cheer. They were on their feet and facing the bleachers, pumping their fists in the air and whipping the crowd into a renewed frenzy.

"You really don't want to do this," I said by way of warning when the female warrior rolled in my direction.

"Big words from such a puny...creature," the Valkyrie scoffed.

"To quote a very wise Muppet, judge me by my size do you?" I really needed to work on my Yoda impersonation; I sounded more like a constipated Gonzo.

"Then face me and prepare to meet whatever maker you subscribe to, Ava Birch."

I felt the slight tugging sensation as the smell and taste of fresh cut grass flooded me. I already knew who was once again present before she said a single word.

"Step away from them!" the voice called in a sweet melodic tone that would have made Aoife proud.

I'm Still Standing

The gate to the arena opened and the elf skated in with more of the grace you would expect from a figure skater than a roller derby queen. Her emerald green hair was a banner streaming behind her as she rolled up and came to a stop just a few feet away.

"You!" the Valkyrie breathed.

Once again I was forgotten like a bag of socks on Christmas morning. The Valkyrie turned to face the elven woman, but she was being awfully cautious. Considering the way they'd rumbled with the Hellbound Foxes and this one was about to square off with Eileen, this was quite a surprise.

What do you know of elves? Blodwen called from someplace deep within my mind.

I had to admit that I didn't know diddly. Not that such things were uncommon, but the fact that I was going to have to play catch up was no biggie; just more of the usual.

They are very skilled in the arts of magic and battle. Most elves are schooled in the use of at least five hand-to-hand weapons as well as the bow and the sling, Blodwen began her brief lecture.

Magic? Like Samantha from Bewitched?

Not exactly, but in many ways, far more potent. They have been known to command the elements of earth and water with incredible might.

That was worth remembering. But, for now, I had a situation that required my full attention. Yay me for not getting side-tracked during the important stuff!

"You will withdraw from this place immediately. If you wish to meet me in single battle, then choose your champion and we shall indeed meet away from the eyes of mortals." The elf shot a glance at me and obviously tried to convey something in that look. The problem was simply that we didn't know each other well enough for me to pick up on some subtle expression.

"You agree to meet the Valkyrie of our choice?"

I suddenly realized that the arena had gone totally silent. Glancing around, at first I thought that the crowd was merely transfixed by the spectacle unfolding before their eyes. Then I did a double-take.

The entire crowd was frozen, I saw people caught mid-scream, cheer, or taunt. In one instance, a lady had thrown her popcorn and the kernels were hovering in mid-air just as they were about to rain down on the head of a man who was pointing a finger at her in a warning that had obviously been ignored.

"I agree under the rules of the Royal Court terms of engagement," the elf replied with a slight bow of her head.

"Then it is agreed," the Valkyrie said with a smile that was just a little bit on the evil side. "Sisters! We are done here."

With that, the Foxes that were still straddled by a Valkyrie were released and the Valkyries all gathered in a group in the center of the skating area. I noticed that none of the Foxes were reacting to being released; I guess it was up to me to state the obvious.

"Umm…you can't just all get up and leave," I announced rather loudly since it was clear that nobody was paying me the slightest bit of attention. "All these people are not going to be able to reconcile the fact that you all simply just vanished from sight." To emphasize my point I walked over and waved a hand in front of the face of one of the spectators. The woman gave no indication of my presence, her eyes still staring straight ahead. To further illustrate my point, I sauntered over to the trucker hat yay-hoos and slapped each one on the face as hard as I dared. Since I was not entirely sure of my own strength, I didn't really want to leave any of them with a broken jaw. However, as an afterthought I did give the one who had been so verbally dismissive to me a good kick between the legs.

"See?" I turned back to the elf and the Valkyries. "Nothing...no response whatsoever."

"You are a cruel creature," one of the Valkyries said, but I was certain that I heard a hint of approval in her tone. Her next statement caught me completely off guard. "Perhaps you might make a good addition to the Sisters of the Shield."

"Umm...thanks, but I already have a job," I stammered. "Now, if you would all be so kind as to return to the appropriate woman that you were beating senseless and then just make it look like you are done and commence your hasty exits without inflicting any further harm."

The Valkyries looked to one another and then shrugged. Almost like reluctant children sent to clean their rooms they trudged back to the various Foxes still lying prone on the ground. That was when another thought struck me.

"Nose Wart!" I shouted. It was unnecessary as the goblin answered from directly beside me.

"Yes, Just Ava?"

"Before the spell is broken, I want you to identify the women who have suffered the worst of the injuries so that we can get them treated first."

The goblin scampered away and ambled among the carnage like he was a judge at a dog show. He would pause and tilt his head one way then the other before moving on to the next inert figure. The Valkyries began to grow impatient and I had to tell Nose Wart to hurry it up. At last he gave me a nod that let me know he had the women prioritized.

I turned to the elf. "Okay, Kari, go ahead and let these people free from whatever spell you have cast." I saw the look of surprise cross her face, but I also saw something else.

Disapproval?

I bet it has been a good long while since somebody told the

Shamadiel Forest Queen what to do, Blodwen snickered.

What? I snapped inwardly. *Why didn't you tell me she was some sort of queen?*

I haven't seen that child in over five hundred years. I wasn't certain she was Karidilean Qu'Shen until she cast that little spell of hers. I recognized the magic signature, but it still took me a while to place the face since she was but a wee elfling last I saw the girl.

Still... I let that unhappy thought resonate in my head, and then I returned my focus to what was going on around me. I realized that the spell had still not been broken and everybody was glaring at me.

"Perhaps you could heed your own cautions," the elf said with haughtiness that I now recognized as the manner in which a royal person might speak to a commoner. She was gonna learn real fast where she stood in my world view.

Oh, this is going to be priceless, Blodwen snickered.

Shut up, you!

I returned to where I'd been in the ring, not bothering to glance at or even acknowledge the elf as I took my place beside Eileen. The Templar had remained frozen through this entire ordeal as well. Or at least that was what I had assumed until she shot me a sly wink. I guess she did not want her cover blown. *Wow, she thinks fast,* I thought. This had me wondering how long everybody had been frozen before I'd noticed, as well as how much quicker on the ball Eileen had to be compared to yours truly.

The eruption of sound was instant and almost painful to my ears. That was quite a powerful ability. I had to wonder what sort of uses it might be put to by somebody (or something) bent on causing havoc and made a note to ask the elf about the extent of that particular spell. Before I could stop myself, I also fantasized about the sorts of things I might be able to do if I had such a power. One gobble and—

Don't you dare, Ava Birch, Blodwen scolded.

I wouldn't...not really.

A howl of pain from behind me made me spin around. I was

wondering what fresh hell this might be when I saw the trucker hat yay-hoo drop to the ground clutching his nether area. His howl of pain changed to something much wetter as he heaved up the contents of his stomach onto the concrete floor in a loud wretch. His buddies were all rubbing their cheeks and looking around with total confusion etched on their faces.

"You can be nasty," Eileen said out of the corner of her mouth as she stifled a laugh.

"You have no idea," I muttered.

***

"So, you must be the Kari that Morgan sent me here to help become the new regional Psychic."

I was sitting at a corner booth in some seedy all-nite café that still had the stains of the days when people used to smoke in restaurants and think that just having a designated smoking area was doing any favors to the non-smokers in the place. I could go on an entire rant about that argument, but you know which side of the argument you fall on, so I won't bother.

Seated beside me on the window ledge was Nose Wart. Across from me was the elven queen or whatever she claimed to be. In a booth a few feet away were Nancy, Tish, and Devonna. In another booth directly across from them sat four elves; three female and one male. They looked like high schoolers, but Blodwen assured me that they were at least a couple of hundred years old.

I'd secured everybody in my mind extra tight with the exception of Blodwen simply because I thought it might be handy to have her for guidance if things got kooky. I had picked up something from Cody just before I sealed him away. A feeling really. Sadness. I wondered what might be brewing with the young necromancer and told myself to add him to my "honey-do" list.

"You will address me as Karidilean Qu'Shen, or Queen of the Shamadiel Forest." The elven woman glared at me and I wanted to tell her that if she was ever going to be a proper Psychic like Morgan, she would need to learn how to keep all the emotion out of her voice...and face.

"First, if you knew how many so-called queens that I am familiar with, you would realize that I stopped seeing that as a big deal a long time ago. As for your little forest, never heard of it, so, as I see it, you are the queen of two things: Jack...and shit. And Jack left town about two weeks ago, so...no, I'm not impressed."

I wish I'd had my cell phone handy to snap a picture of the look on her face in that moment. It reminded me of the day when the captain of the dance team, Kelly Thompson, this cute, way-too-perky brunette went on her period right in the middle of a pep assembly...wearing a snow white dance team unitard. Hey...funny word. Unitard. Go ahead, say it out loud and try not to giggle just a little.

Ooops!

"...the forest that you know as the Apache-Sitgreaves National Forest, but I assure you, it had a name long before humans gave it a label." She was still staring down her nose at me, but I was already over it. The way I saw the situation, she needed me much more than I needed her.

"Fine, so why leave such posh digs for Dallas? I mean, nothing against the good people of Texas, but I would rather be Queen of the Forest than some regional Psychic." Yay me for the hard-hitting Wolf Blitzer questions.

"There is a war coming, Ava Birch," Kari said with all seriousness. "We will be part of it."

"We? We who?

"The elves of course."

"Yeah, fine. But why do you need to be a Psychic? Why not just join on the side of the good guys and bring your little woodland friends along?" Wow, I may not be the best at how I word things, but I was really feeling proud of the way I was coming at this elven queen with some hardcore questions that went right to the heart of the situation.

"Good guys?" Kari scoffed. "Is that how you see things, Ava Birch? There are no good guys in this war. There are simply two sides that oppose each other's ideas."

I considered that statement for a few seconds and looked over at Nose Wart. His eyes were glued on the vampires. Hmm...no help there.

"Okay, and what do they oppose?" Not my best question during this little meeting, but I was not sure how to find out anything. I was absolutely unprepared for her response.

"Why, has nobody told you?" A smile curved the corners of the pretty elf's lips. "Your existence."

Damn, and me with my mouth empty once again, thus missing another perfect opportunity for a classic spit-take. The fact that I would have sprayed said beverage all over the Forest Queen was simply an added bonus.

"Wait, let me get this straight. This war that I keep hearing about is because of me? Why? What did I ever do?"

"Your very existence is a threat, Ava Birch. But there are those who believe that it is you who might bring us into the light."

I reached up and used my index finger to shut my mouth which had dropped open wide. "Bring you into the light? Hold the phone. If this is some sort of cult thing or spiritual whatever, I am not the ghoul you are looking for. I can barely lead a sing-a-long; much less lead anybody or anything into the light."

"You are the one in the prophecy, there is almost no doubt."

"Umm...ex-squeeze me? Baking powder? What the hell prophecy are you talking about?"

Karidilean Qu'Shen, the Regal and Exalted Queen of the Shamadiel Forest snapped her fingers. One of the female elves popped up from her seat which caused Nancy to do the same. I gave her a gesture with my hand indicating it was okay and that she could sit back down. I saw actual worry on her face, but she did as I requested.

The female elf came to the table and produced an ancient looking scroll and began to read. "She will rise again in a pure form and be divested of the human nature, yet she will cling to it. It is this undead creature that will step forward before humanity and lead all the extraordinary children to the light where they will join once more in the life so decreed before the Great Banishment."

"Okay, here is where I ask all my stupid questions," I huffed. "Let's start with this Great Banishment. It sounds important."

"It was the day that all of us non-humans were decreed to remove ourselves from the general population of Mother Earth." Queen Kari got a faraway look in her eyes. "My grandmother tells of the days when the whole world was a glorious mix of human and what is now deemed Supernatural. Sadly, as the humans became more aware of themselves, they also realized their limitations. Jealousy became a deep-seated fear and hatred, and we were eventually banished from society as a whole by the human known as Emperor Frederick II in the year 1215."

"Okay...hold on again. That was almost eleven hundred years after Boudicca, this supposed ghoul that everybody talks about in hushed whispers."

"That was her human years. Boudicca lived for centuries after that. There are even rumors that she continues to exist and that the tales of her defeat are simply lies spread by the Augustines and the Templars to pacify those who fear her name to this day," Queen Kari explained.

"You guys don't do anything easy, do ya?" I grumbled.

""We could go on about history for hours and days, Ava Birch, but the time for that must be later. At the moment, we have greater concerns and issues that need attending."

"Like me taking down Claude the Psychic and then handing the district over to you?" I leaned across the table and fixed the elven queen with my hardest stare. "Maybe you should tell me the real reason why you want this district and why it was so important that I come here and take care of your business. I saw your archers, and you seem to have plenty of warrior types that could handle this for you."

"That would not remove your claim from this region. The day would eventually come when we would have to square off and settle your claim to this territory," Kari lectured.

"So we handle it in a non-lethal matter then. Why the push

to get me here and do all of this stuff right now?"

"You are still coming into your powers, Ava Birch," Kari said slowly after a very long pause where I could tell she was trying to figure out exactly what to tell me and what to withhold. "You might crave power when you get more established. That could encourage you to challenge me in a lethal manner, in which case there is no doubt that I would lose."

"Wow, you don't have a very high opinion of your abilities," I scoffed.

"No, I simply have a very high opinion of yours."

That statement hung in the air for a few heartbeats. I was unsure how to respond, but thankfully, Nancy came to the table. "The sun will be making its appearance soon, Ava. We need to be going."

I scooted out of the booth and gave Queen Kari a nod. "I will meet you at Claude's tomorrow night. We will handle that little bit of business so I can cross it off my list."

"Actually," the elf made no move to stand, but she fixed me with her gaze and I saw something flash in her eyes that could have been fear, "I need your help in one other matter."

"You don't think that me obtaining the Dallas region for you to take over as Psychic is enough?"

Tread careful, Ava, Blodwen warned.

That simple warning made my fingertips and toes tingle. If the gwyll was concerned, then I was definitely nervous.

"There is the matter of the Valkyries." Now Queen Kari made it a point to slip out of the booth and stand. I didn't know if it was an elven thing, or something else, but she was standing really close...like WAY up in my personal space. Then she did something that caused Blodwen to gasp audibly in my head.

Karidilean Qu'Shen, Queen of the Shamadiel Forest, knelt before me and placed her forehead on my booted left foot. She kept her face down, but her words rang clear. "I beseech you, Ava Birch, revered ghoul and she who is spoken of in the ancient prophecies, please act as my champion."

Oh my, Blodwen breathed. *This is quite an honor as well as an amazing opportunity. You would be advised to accept her plea.*

"Umm…okay," I finally said when I realized that the elf hadn't moved since making her request.

It was then that I also noticed the other elves in her party had moved to the aisle and joined their queen. Personally, I was actually having more trouble reconciling the fact that this queen had just knelt on the floor of an all-night diner. Seriously….gross!

"Then we must meet at the location appointed by the Valkyries. As soon as it is revealed, I will send one of my messengers to inform you of the time, place, and any stipulations. Although, with them being Valkyries, I doubt there will be any restrictions. That actually bodes better for us. If they make no demands, then you will be free to fight in the manner you find most comfortable."

"Say what?" I blurted.

"Oh, Just Ava, this is truly going to be something to tell the clan when we return home." Nose Wart was bouncing up and down like a three-year-old who had just devoured an entire one pound bag of M & Ms.

"Hold the phone, everybody." I raised my hand to put an end to the sudden onslaught of jabbering that came from not only Nose Wart, but also the vampires and all of the elves in Queen Kari's contingent. "To quote the diminutive Arnold Drummond…whatchoo talkin' 'bout, Willis?"

9

You Dropped a Bomb on Me

"You will be the champion of an elven queen," Nose Wart breathed in reverence and a little too much awe for my liking.

"You mind telling me what the hell that means?" I grabbed Queen Kari by the arm and hauled her to her feet. Yeah, she might've shot me a withering glare, but my Give-A-Damn meter had broken a long time ago, and I doubted there would be any repairs in the near (or distant) future.

"You will be an extension of me in the battle with the Valkyrie."

You know, she said that like it was the most natural thing in the whole world. *I need you to grab some milk and eggs from the store, oh…and fight a Valkyrie on your way back*. I heard that so clearly in my head that I was almost convinced that it was Blodwen, but then I realized she was taking this precise moment to be mute.

Hey! I yelled inwardly. *How about a little help here!*

You seem to be handling things exceptionally well, Blodwen broke her silence to utter those useless words of encouragement.

"We should receive the official challenge and the rules of combat very soon." Queen Kari brushed herself off and motioned for entourage to get to their feet.

"So, what do I get?" It wasn't exactly a greedy question as much as it was my own curiosity. I mean, what could an elven queen offer me besides money? I bet it was going to be something really cool. I was sure hoping that to be the case considering I'd seen these Valkyries in limited combat. They were nasty and exceedingly tough. A full-on battle would probably be very nasty.

"You shall be proclaimed as my champion," Queen Kari said with a degree of enthusiasm that let me know that was supposed to be a big deal. Now I gotta quote Bugs Bunny: *"She don't know me very well...do she?"*

"Yeah...that's sweet. But what does that do for me? I mean, I realize you have been away from the human realm for a while, but I am pretty sure that you know the concept of what a bank will allow me to deposit. It's not like I can stroll up to the teller and say I am depositing my title of champion." Yikes, that sounded a bit snottier than I'd intended. And when did I become so money hungry? That wasn't like me at all. Was it?

"You shall be allowed freedom whenever you are within my realm. In addition, you will have your choice of consorts provided they are not of royal blood." As the queen spoke, I saw the looks of longing and perhaps a bit of envy cast shadows over the faces of the female elves that were in her little band of followers.

"So I can visit whenever I want and I can bump uglies with my choice of your male elven population." I gave a shrug. "Nice. Not thrilling...but nice." I think I heard Dom DeLuise utter that line in the part of my mind not already occupied by a bunch of Supernaturals. He was dressed as Julius Ceasar...and if you have no idea what I am talking about...you have my pity.

"Your choices are not restricted to the males if that is your preference," Queen Kari amended a bit hastily.

"Not exactly my thing, but I'll keep it in mind if I ever decide to wander down the Katy Perry expressway."

"And you shall be granted a keep of our best craftsmanship."

That earned gasps from Nose Wart, Blodwen, Nancy, Tish, and Devonna as well as double-takes from the elves. Something told me that she'd just sweetened the pot with the grand prize. I had to really be missing something since all I heard was "blah-blah...elf sex...blah-blah...house."

An elven keep is a fortress of incredible beauty and quite a treasure indeed, Blodwen informed me.

But I already have a house, I groaned inwardly. *I don't want to move again. And besides, I imagine it is built in that forest place she is the queen of. I don't want some castle in the woods.*

Actually, I am certain that it would be built in the location of your choosing, Blodwen explained.

But why do I need a keep or whatever the hell she is offering that has everybody in such a tizzy?

Considering your recent issues with this offshoot Templar group, I think a keep may be just the thing to ensure not only your safety, but also that of all who may come to follow you in the future, Blodwen replied, sounding like she was actually pacing the floor and giving this keep some serious thought in regards to its benefits.

Okay, but won't a keep take months if not years to construct?

That is the beauty of earth magic. The construction could likely be done within days. Add in a few extra days for the wards and enchantments to be put in place and I would wager your keep fully functional within a month.

Queen Kari cleared her throat, and I realized that I'd been carrying on this entire conversation inside my head while she stood waiting for me to reply. I gave a shrug.

"What the heck, I was already sent here and hired to take care of these Valkyries, I'll call your little offer a bonus." With that, I motioned for Nose Wart to follow me as I made for the exit. I had to hide a smile as Queen Kari practically choked when I said I'd accept her "little offer" as a bonus.

"Why did you mock the queen?" Nancy hissed as we climbed into the car. "She has given you a great and rich offer."

"I didn't mock anybody, but saying that I have freedom while in her realm? Not a thing. And giving me my choice of consorts? Do I strike you as a gal who can't land a guy with her own wiles?"

Okay, so maybe I wasn't exactly tearing up the world in regards to my sex life as of late. But still, I am far from needing to be somebody's charity lay.

"Do you even comprehend what an elven keep could mean?" Nancy scolded.

"Umm…I'm gonna go with no as my final answer."

"Between the magical wards and elven security features, you would be able to withstand just about anything thrown at you," Nancy said in a rapid fire response that almost devoured her Southern accent with the speed in which her words flew at me. "She is basically offering you the start to your own kingdom if you choose."

"Yeah, well, I don't want a kingdom." I had a hard time keeping my voice level for some reason. It was odd, but all of this started to seem just a bit too convenient. I had a feeling that Morgan's fingerprints were all over this if I looked hard enough.

I puzzled over my emotions for a moment. It was as if I was being given everything I needed, so why was I so miffed? It wasn't as if I believed that I could handle everything being thrown at me all by myself, but at the same time, I did not feel like I had reached a point where I needed people going out of their way to try and protect me.

When did I become the one needing to be saved?

"Oh my," Nancy gasped as she took a step back.

My head snapped up and I regarded the vampire and her two female companions with curiosity. I glanced down, following her gaze and realized that my fingers and toes had gone switch on me. I did not need a mirror to confirm that I was also in Sharkmouth mode.

"If we have offended you—" Nancy began to stammer.

"No!" I snapped a bit more gruffly than I intended. "You have done nothing. I just need to be left alone for a little while."

Hmm…when had we gotten home to Nancy's place?

"As you wish." The trio headed for the stairs and Nancy called over her shoulder as she exited, "A fresh corpse is in the cabinet just behind you."

I glanced down to see Nose Wart continuing to stand at my side. He looked up at me and then bowed at the waist.

"Shall I fetch your meal, Just Ava?"

"No. Perhaps you should join the vampires."

"And leave you?"

"Maybe it would be best for now." I gave a dismissive wave of my hand as I stalked over to the cabinet and pulled out the relatively fresh corpse. I was about to start eating when I heard a throat clear behind me. I turned to discover the goblin standing at rigid attention, gnarled hands pressed at his side.

"If I have failed you, mistress, I shall atone. If I am displeasing, then you may feel free to consume me and choose another member of the Goblin Vomit clan to assume the role of chieftain."

"What?" I barked. "Why would I eat you? What could you have done that you need to atone for?"

"I did not attend you properly at the meeting with Karidilean Qu'Shen, Queen of the Shamadiel Forest. My eyes and focus were not on you and something has occurred that I obviously was not aware of. It has caused you some distress, and since I was not paying attention, I obviously missed it and have therefore failed you."

There is something wrong, Ava, Blodwen and Butt Pimple both said almost in perfect unison.

It is as if something is fighting for control of this space, Blodwen explained. *While it certainly feels like you, there is something about the patterns of your mind that are trying to alter...change.*

Something is trying to control my mind? I asked, unsure of what exactly the old gwyll was trying to say.

In a matter of speaking.

It is hostile and dark, Butt Pimple chimed in.

"I don't have time for this crap," I snarled out loud. "Between having to fight a Valkyrie, take down a Psychic, and keep my eyes open for renegade Templars, I am reaching a point where I don't think I can take another thing going wrong in my life."

"But you are a ghoul," Nose Wart said as if that was the answer to every single one of my problems. "You are Just Ava, vanquisher of Prince Fraylee, destroyer of a lamia, bane of vampires, crippler of jötunn, and slayer of lake trolls."

When he said all those things together, I guess it sounded a little impressive. Granted, it would never fit on a business card, but if I was writing a resume, I did have a fairly impressive list of achievements in a relatively short period of time.

I was about to thank the little goblin for the pep talk when horrific screaming came from inside my head. It was so sudden and strong that I had no recollection of dropping to my knees. Yet, when I was able to open my eyes again and focus, I was staring eye-to-eye with Nose Wart. His worry was evident and etched hard across his face.

"What is it?" he whispered, looking around as if he might be able to discover some hidden attacker.

Just then, another scream came from inside my head, but this time it was followed by a tremendous howl. There was fury and rage in that sound. Only, instead of that noise adding to my discomfort, it flooded me with the desire to kill and feed. It was almost like *Fame Rabia*, but that was impossible. I had not suffered any serious damage, and I still had plenty of time remaining before I absolutely had to feed. Oh, and there was this fresh corpse right in front of me.

Not wanting to risk anything, I tore into my meal. My head had gone totally silent the moment I began to feed. I tried to call out for Blodwen, Butt Pimple…hell I even called for Cody, Mystify, and Adrianna. I received no replies from any of them. Even more concerning, I could not sense anything in my mind other than a knot of dark anger and hatred.

I finished eating, and glanced over to see Nose Wart pacing nervously near the steps. He cocked his head when I looked at him and began to inch closer to me, his eyes locked on mine.

"What?" The way he was looking at me was becoming unsettling. It was as if he might be studying me, and I could see him becoming more agitated by the second.

"There is a shadow inside you," he breathed.

I looked everywhere for a mirror and then realized that I was in the basement of vampires. Why not look for some garlic and a tub of holy water while I was at it?

"Get over here." I pointed to the spot right in front of me. Nose Wart dutifully scurried over. I leaned close, doing all I could to hold my eyes as wide open as possible. "Look into my eyes."

He did so and then staggered back as if struck. "My precious Butt Pimple." He blinked and I swore that a milky tear formed in the corner of his left eye. His hands scrubbed at his face and wiped away any evidence of what I may or may not have seen.

"What?" I implored. "What is it, Nose Wart?"

His little head swung up to me, and for a second, I saw recrimination. But once again, he pushed aside whatever he was feeling and met my gaze. However, I was seeing something different in his face.

It reminded me of this good friend I had in my freshman year back when I was still awkward and flat chested. Her name was Crissy Worton and we were besties before that was even a word. But then Karl Soderman came along. He was sweet and Crissy crushed hard on him. Since she declared her crush first, our friendship code meant that he was instantly off limits for me. Only, she moved away to Tucson the summer between our freshman and sophomore year. Fast forward a few months where Karl and I run into each other at a little party. One thing led to another and...well...I probably don't need to give you the details.

Seriously, Crissy was in freakin' Arizona. How was I supposed to know that her family would move back the very next year just in time to make junior year VERY awkward. Her crush came on in full force the first time she and Karl crossed paths, unfortunately, Karl and I had already moved on and were not exactly on speaking terms. (You remember high school breakups…they almost never ended in friendship.) Crissy and I were never the same. Of course it didn't help that my popularity meter had swung in a different direction while she remained the shy, quiet wallflower she'd been back when we were so close.

Anyway, Nose Wart was looking at me in much the same way Crissy had the day she discovered that Karl and I had been a thing for a few weeks. I had no idea that goblins were capable of so many normal feelings.

"What do you see?" I demanded.

"Sh-she has been flayed and is hanging from a rack," Nose Wart managed.

"How?" I gasped.

"Did she displease you, Just Ava?"

"Did she…what? No!" I stammered. "And even if she did, why would I do something like that?"

"You are a ghoul."

Once again, there was a statement being made about my supposed nature as if the word "ghoul" was all that needed to be said in explanation. I know I keep saying it, but I really do need to get my hands on some in-depth information about the history of ghouls.

"I didn't do anything to her, Nose Wart." I grabbed his chin and made him look at me since he was suddenly finding something very interesting at his feet. "And can you see anything else? Is there anybody else in there who has been…did you say flayed?" He nodded. "Yes, flayed? Or yes you can see somebody else?"

"I only see my beloved." There was a pause, and then he said one more thing that gave me a bit of a chill. "And the shadows."

"What shadows?"

He shrugged and shook his head. "It is simply a shadow, but there is nothing casting it as it moves."

I didn't like this at all. There was something in my head that was apparently wreaking havoc on the current residents. And just moments before, Blodwen had said something about there being a problem, like there was a dark presence trying to take control of my mind or some such nonsense.

Whatever it was, I could feel it. My mind flashed to a few other times when I'd acted out of my normal character and wondered what had caused it. Was there some Supernatural inside me that I'd consumed perhaps during my Fame Rabia? Or was this something from the lamia? I was never totally clear about which Supernaturals could take up residence in my head after I took them down. Did I have to completely consume them, or was it something activated by my having beaten them in a fight?

"Is she gone?" Nose Wart whispered, snapping me back to it.

"Is who gone?" I asked, shaking my head to try and clear whatever was floating around in there.

"Butt Pimple. Did you dispose of her?"

"Nose Wart, for the last time, I didn't do anything to her." He simply bowed his head. That pissed me off even more and I grabbed him by the face once again, wrenching his head up so that he had to look me in the eyes. "Have I ever lied to you before?" He shook his head a fraction of a centimeter which was sort of impressive considering the grip I had on his face. "So why would I lie to you about this?"

He looked at me, and I swear I saw the clouds part in his expression. "You would not, Just Ava." He pulled back and I let go. Instantly, he flung himself at my feet. "Please forgive me. You have never treated me harshly or unkind. I am shamed for doubting you."

"Again, this is something that we can do later. Right now we need to figure out what is going on in my head." I wonder how many guys in my life have asked that same question.

I took two steps when I heard a low sinister laugh…from inside my head. I couldn't help but flash back to that cheesy slasher flick, *When a Stranger Calls*. This was not a voice or a laugh that I recognized, and there was absolutely nothing friendly about that laugh. And even worse…I could feel whatever it was! It was mean and nasty and ugly.

So this is what has become of ghouls, a harsh and raspy voice that I was only partially certain belonged to a female barked from inside my head.

"Boudicca?"

10

Harden My Heart

I did the only thing I could think of; I went on mental lockdown. I used everything I'd ever learned when dealing with Adrianna and Mystify and attempted to shut away what I was now almost absolutely certain had to somehow be the spirit or essence of the last great female ghoul.

Boudicca was the reason that the Templars had been commissioned to eliminate all of ghoulkind. Basically, she was bad news. I had no idea how she had suddenly popped into my head, but I knew that she'd already done terrible things to Butt Pimple and I had to guess that Blodwen at the very least had suffered a similar fate. Unfortunately, I was not sure if it was permanent. Could I undo what had been done?

That would have to come later. Right now, I needed to shut her away. I felt wall after wall smashed aside like nothing. My attempts at securing her only seemed to make her angrier and more determined to assert herself.

Foolish girl! The presence roared after smashing aside another of my attempted barriers. Something clicked in my head in a flash and I knew it was coming from one of my mental residents. I didn't know which one, but I grabbed hold of that idea and wove what amounted to a very dense and sticky web around the core of darkness that rampaged around my head. I repeated that exercise another three times and then brought on the strong-est box I could think of to finally lock away the malevolence.

"Just Ava, are you okay?" Nose Wart shouted. From the looks and sound of my little goblin friend, he'd been trying to get my attention for quite some time.

"Ava?" I heard Nancy calling from above. "Is there any-thing we can do? Do we dare come down?"

I took a deep breath and then did an internal check to make sure things were at least partially settled. My box was hold-ing...at least for now. Just for good measure, I invoked that mysterious web spell and secured the box in place. I still could not pin down any readings on Blodwen, Butt Pimple, or any of the others, but I knew that somebody in there had just pulled my little gray butt out of the fire.

"It's okay," I called out.

A second later, the door to the cellar opened, and with their vampire quickness, all three female vamps were spread out in front of me. It was clear that they were remaining cautious; even Tish had a look of concern etched on her smooth features in place of her normal scowl.

"You were shrouded in shadow, Just Ava," Nose Wart re-ported, stepping up to me and obviously trying to peer into my eyes. I looked down to facilitate his attempt and saw him cringe. Obviously things were still in disarray in my head.

"What do you mean?" I asked, unsure of what he was talk-ing about.

"A dark shadow that not even my vision could penetrate en-veloped you and then there were dark flashes of ugly purples and greens like lightning that crackled and arced along that dark-ness," the goblin explained. "I tried to touch you once and it flung me across the room."

"I'm so sorry," I apologized.

"Yes, and all the lights went out," Devonna added. "Of course it was actually quite fortuitous since this all took place when the messenger from the elves arrived with word of the time and place of your battle."

"Good news on that front," Nancy picked up the narrative. "There are no restrictions other than the total exclusion of magic. Since your abilities are inherent, you will have full use of your ghoulish powers."

"Yay?" I didn't really know how to respond to this newest development. Honestly, the Valkyrie was now the least of my concerns. I had the grandmother of all female ghouls trapped in my head with no idea how she got there and no clue as to how I would be able to keep her under control.

"Also, one of the young ladies from the roller derby team has arrived and is waiting to speak with you," Nancy finished.

"Okay, but I think I am going to need to feed again as soon as you can arrange it. I have no idea what sort of toll that little incident has taken on me and I can't afford to lose control right now." I walked over to a sofa against the wall and plopped down.

I felt tired, and that was saying something since I NEVER felt tired. Hungry? Yes. Tired? Nope…not since the day I'd become a ghoul.

Nancy made a wave of her hand and Devonna vanished up the stairs. Tish stayed put, and I noticed that she was almost clinging to Nancy's side. I guess I hadn't really thought of it up until now, but I had to guess that she was Nancy's chief protector or whatever vampires call them.

"Dare I ask what has happened?" Nancy asked almost timidly.

I shrugged, seeing no reason for this to be a secret. It was probably not normal in the Supernatural world to reveal these sorts of things, but I personally saw no reason for all the secrets and hoarding of information.

"That sounds serious," the vampire said once I finished sharing all of what I figured to be the pertinent details.

"Yes, well, I need to start getting some of the stuff crossed off my list before I can deal with whatever this fresh turn of events has in store for me." I looked past Nancy as a pair of legs came down to the basement.

I was not entirely surprised to see that Eileen was the representative from the roller derby team that had come to see me. She had a look on her face that told me I was either going to hate whatever she had to say, or else she was about to add yet another item to my growing list of things I needed to attend to in the near or immediate future.

Yay…it turned out to be both.

"We only know that it was a vampire, and that he took Brandy."

"What the hell is wrong here in Texas?" I snapped.

It sure doesn't seem like we have all this out-of-control Supernatural crap going on back home. Or maybe I was simply oblivious except for what Morgan chose to share.

"This has to be Claude's doing," I said, making nothing more than a silly-wild-ass-guess.

"The regional Psychic?" Eileen sounded dubious. "I would think he might be more concerned with keeping his territory in order."

"Not if he is fearing for his life," I muttered.

"Why would he fear for his life?" Eileen asked slowly as if she feared having her suspicion in regards to my answer being confirmed.

"Are you sure that you want to know?" I fixed her with a very cold stare; or at least that was what I was shooting for.

The sound of somebody pounding on the door cut off her chance to reply. Nancy actually looked startled and Tish popped fangs as her head snapped around.

"Impossible," Nancy breathed.

"Oh jeez!" I blurted. "What now?"

"There is an elven contingent at our door." Nancy actually sounded awestruck. She crept up the stairs and vanished from sight.

"Probably just some of Queen Kari's people," I said with a shrug, not seeing what the big deal might be over a few visiting elves.

"Umm, elves don't usually make it a habit to call on vampires," Eileen explained. "They are like crack to the bloodsuckers." Tish hissed and took a menacing step toward the Templar who threw up her hands. "Sorry...old habit." Eileen looked to me and clarified. "That is a derogatory term in vamp circles."

"You have GOT to be kidding." I couldn't help it. I started laughing. Pretty soon I was doubled over, clutching at my belly. The scowls I received from Tish and even Devonna only made me laugh harder.

"I fail to see what is so funny," Devonna said with a pout that looked amazingly adorable on her face.

"Political correctness has seeped into the Supernatural world." It actually took me a few seconds to say that as I simply could not stop laughing at the absurdity of the situation.

"I'd like to see how you felt if she called you a corpse eater," Devonna protested.

"Big, fat, hairy deal." I shrugged my shoulders. "Knock yourself out."

"Are you not offended?" Devonna took a step closer to me, tilting her head in curiosity.

"I have bigger things to worry about other than labels. Besides, they only have power as long as you give it. Otherwise, it is simply like the old adage of sticks-and-stones."

"Ava!" Nancy called as she hurried down the stairs. "Please tell these...these...*elves* that you are not in need of their service as bodyguards. We are quite capable of keeping you out of danger and ensuring that you arrive on time for your duel."

Three elves followed on the blonde vampire's heels. All three were female and dressed in what looked like paper-thin metallic armor. Seriously, I'd seen thicker sheets of aluminum foil. The armor was molded to their tall, slender bodies and I was at least thankful that they were not spilling up and out of their breastplates; none of them had much more than a handful at the most.

The one in the lead had snow white skin and hair the color of spun silver with lavender eyes that sparkled as she took in the room with a military keenness. I could tell that she had quickly determined every threat and logged every detail of this space.

Her eyes dwelled the longest on Nose Wart and the slightest scowl of disdain curved her thin lips down for a second before she dismissed the appearance of the goblin to just another factor of the room should a fight break out.

The two standing on their leader's flanks had hair that was grass green. Their eyes matched in their emerald iridescence and both were a shade of light brown that was more like a tree trunk and not a normal shade you would find on any human. Each had her hand on the hilt of the blade hanging conspicuously at their right hip.

"What on earth would make you think that I need guarding?" I huffed as I rose to my feet to confront the elves and put myself in a position between them and the vampires just in case somebody got antsy.

"We were dispatched by our queen and do as we are bid," the leader replied.

"Yes, well...I don't need your protection, and I think it might be best if you return to your queen and tell her that I am more than capable of taking care of myself."

"We will not disobey our queen," the elf insisted without any hint of emotion. She was stating it as a fact. End of discussion.

"Yeah, well I am telling you that, as her champion, I don't need you here and demand that you leave."

"We will withdraw outside, but we shall remain here and we will accompany you to the location chosen for the battle."

With that, the three elves turned and marched up the stairs. I felt the being within my head make a new surge at trying to free herself/itself from my confinement. I hastily threw another web at the containment and returned my attention to Nancy and the other two vampires.

"So, we have a time and a place. But what is the deal with you and the elves?" I ran my hands through my hair and tried to find a sense of calm with the hopes that relaxing would allow me to gain some much needed control over this crazy situation.

"It is next to impossible for us to resist the allure of elven blood. It is an elixir that surpasses even that of a faerie," Nancy explained. "I would have only been able to restrain myself for a limited amount of time before succumbing to my desires."

"And are elves aware of your position in this matter?" I asked, sounding tired to my own ears.

"Quite," Tish spoke up. "Elves are some of the most notorious vampire hunters. They lure us out by actually using themselves as bait. That has made us natural enemies for well over a thousand years."

"So why would these three simply stroll into your house?"

"Because they were sent by their queen…and elves do not fear vampires." This time it was Devonna stepping forward with the answers after the other two exchanged what I took as nervous glances.

"Yeah, I really need to get my hands on that stupid *Grimoire*," I muttered. I paused, almost certain that I heard a soft moan or whimper from within my head. I waited a few seconds, but there was nothing.

"If you don't mind, Ava, we need to retire to our sleeping area," Nancy said.

She and the other two vampires headed back up the stairs followed by Eileen who gave a casual shrug and wave, leaving me and Nose Wart alone. I glanced at the goblin and was not surprised to see him openly staring at me.

"See anything?" I asked, plopping down on the floor to be more at his level. The goblin shook his head.

Despite the fact that he was staring directly at me, I knew he wasn't exactly looking at me. His eyes were locked on mine, but he was staring past the surface and into me. Any other time in my past, that might have bothered me, but at this moment, I actually felt a sense of peace knowing that the little guy was watching me. It didn't matter that he was not actually watching me per se. I knew very well that he was monitoring what he saw inside my eyes. I wondered if perhaps this ability was tied to the same power that had allowed him to see that Brandy was bleeding internally.

That got my mind back to the fact that some vampire had snatched up Brandy from the hospital. If gambling were my thing, I would probably bet that the revenants Eileen, Nose Wart, and I had dealt with were under the control of the same vamp that kidnapped Brandy. My next missing puzzle piece had to do with why exactly a vampire would grab the woman in the first place.

"You can be so stupid, Ava!" I blurted.

In one of our first conversations, Brandy had said something about the fact that her sister was a thrall to a vampire. I was pretty sure that she had said that his name was Hector. I was now guessing that this had something to do with everything.

"Wow…just like a real mystery," I mused.

"What?" Nose Wart shook himself and actually focused on my face instead of just staring into my eyes.

"I was just saying how this was actually starting to shape up like one of those silly books. You have a whole bunch of things that are seemingly unrelated, but by the end, the hero of the story wins the day and solves the problems as it is discovered how a series of random things are all part of the Big Picture."

I just knew that Chantal was going to love this provided I managed to actually solve anything and stay alive. Not only that, but maybe my critics, those readers that keep saying these stories never go anywhere, will finally be satisfied. (I'm looking at you Shondra from Florida!)

***

"And you have never heard of a vampire in this area by the name of Hector?" I asked Nancy for what was probably the fourth or fifth time as I paced back and forth in the living room while we waited for Tish and Devonna to gather everything they felt they needed for this little excursion.

"Not in this region. We are the only three vampires in this Kiss. I have not been very excited about adding to our numbers simply because of the politics. With it just being the three of us, we all have our roles and are happy with things as they are," Nancy explained.

"Okay, so how do you know that other vampires are not moving in on your territory?" I pressed.

"The Psychic would inform us and we would have to either meet them in battle or merge as one group."

"And you have no reason to think Claude is up to something sneaky?"

"He leaves us alone. We know that he has a few revenants that serve him in his residence, but he brought those in from the last region he lived and made sure to declare them to us."

"Yeah...well something is fishy here. Brandy said that her sister was a thrall for a vampire named Hector."

This little revelation obviously had the vampires bothered. I may not know much about the vampire community (or anything Supernatural for that matter), but I know enough of the basics to realize that this was a big deal. I was now more certain than ever that this was part of the whole picture. I also believed that Claude was the heart of this matter, and if I could rip him out of the situation, it might solve a great many things.

"It is time, ghoul!" a voice called from outside.

"Damn," I swore under my breath. It would have been nice to try and take out what I considered to be the easiest target first, but I would have to take things as they came.

I turned to Nose Wart. He was ready for war and had his nasty little sword in his hand. His face was set in a look of grim determination and I knew he was not going to like the next words out of my mouth.

"I need you to do me a favor, Nose Wart."

I knelt in front of the goblin and placed my hands on his knobby shoulders. He simply looked up at me and nodded. I knew that he would do anything I asked. His loyalty to me, no matter how unfounded it may be considering the fact that I'd really done nothing to deserve it, would prompt him to act on my commands without question whether he liked it or not.

"I need you to go to Claude's house and keep an eye on it. If anything comes or goes, you keep track so that when I arrive I have an idea of what to expect."

"But who will be at your side when you face the Valkyrie?" he asked solemnly. I could tell he was conflicted. He saw his role in my life as being my constant protector whether I needed it or not.

"I will be there to watch her back," Nancy said softly. "I promise you, little goblin, there will be no surprises."

"And I will be going with you," Devonna spoke up, stepping beside Nose Wart.

This earned a reaction from everybody. I simply smiled because I thought it was cute. Tish looked appalled, and Nancy seemed only mildly surprised, but very amused. None of us were blind; although I don't think I would be able to say the same about blooming love. It never seems to strike where you expect, and, more often than not, hits hardest where you least anticipate.

Devonna probably would have blushed, if she'd been able, when all eyes turned to her. Still, she straightened and then hastily added, "If there is a vampire in this territory, it is a certainty that the Psychic is aware. That might be something we need to be prepared for, my friends."

Nancy and Tish both seemed to accept that reason as appropriate. Then they did something that, try as I might, I could never picture Belinda doing with any of the vampires in her Kiss: they hugged.

"If we are late, it is a forfeit," an angry elven voice called down.

"I'm coming, keep your shirt on." I stood, giving Nose Wart a pat on the shoulder. "You be careful and don't do anything foolish. That means you stay out of sight until I arrive. Understand?"

"Yes, Just Ava." Nose Wart bowed and then gave me a salute with his sword.

I headed for the stairs with Nancy and Tish on my heels. I stepped outside to discover a windowless panel van parked in front of the house. The side door was open and one of the elves stood beside it, gesturing impatiently for us to hurry up. We piled in and the vehicle lurched forward with a slam of the door and the squeal of tires.

It was time to put on my game face. I was about to fight a Valkyrie to the death. As that thought came, I felt the dark presence in my head almost grow calm. It was as if my mentally preparing for a fight was some sort of soothing tonic to what I was now almost certain had to be Boudicca...or her spirit...or whatever the hell piece of her had found residence in my head.

I was almost about to allow myself to feel some relief when a surge of something coursed through me. I fought to control it. She was not breaking free, but it was as if she might be channeling something into me. Something dark.

I struggled to contain it, but it was like a sand castle being washed away by the tide. I could feel parts of me...Ava Birch...sort of melting away. Only, unlike the hypothetical sand castle, instead of everything being washed away and leaving nothing, I could feel something else rising up to take its place.

I could not keep my lips from curving into a smile. My fingers and toes switched and I felt my mouth grow wide as Sharkmouth came.

"By the goddess," the elf that had been sitting next to me gasped as he slowly moved away.

Nancy glanced over her shoulder and her eyes went wide with what I had to guess was actual fear. "Ava?"

I had to swallow twice before my mouth would form the word, but at last I was finally able to acknowledge her. "Yes."

Hmm, I thought, *that sure didn't sound like my voice. That almost sounded like...Boudicca.*

That Ghoul Ava on a Roll!

11

Is There Something I Should Know

"Your skin," Tish gasped.

I glanced down at my hands and was a little surprised to see jet black tracers lacing my arms. "That's new," I sputtered.

The van came to a stop and the elf beside me practically fell over himself trying to get to the sliding side door and yank it open so that he could put some distance between he and I. Interestingly enough, Tish was right on his heels. Nancy was the only one to remain and she was staring at me with open concern.

"Has that ever happened before?" she asked in a remarkably calm voice.

"Nope." Once again I was a bit startled that the voice coming out of my mouth did not sound as much like me as it did Boudicca. Was I possessed?

"Any idea as to what it might be?"

"Actually…" I leaned forward so that my eyes were only inches away from hers. "Do you see anything when you look into my eyes?"

Nancy was a real trooper. I mean, she could just as easily moved away from me; but instead, she actually leaned in to me and peered directly into my eyes. After a few seconds, she sat back and shook her head.

"Sorry, Ava, all I see is your solid black eyes."

"Yes, well I have a feeling that I might be possessed or something."

"That isn't possible," Nancy stated matter-of-factly.

"Oh? And why is that?"

"You no longer have your soul."

Take a second with me and digest that little nugget. The first thing that came to my mind was that this would actually be some sort of acknowledgement or confirmation that I once had a soul. Wouldn't the theologists love to hear that little tidbit of information? Of course there was now the very unpleasant realization that I no longer had one. I was not very happy about that, but I did not have to stew over it too long before Nancy continued.

"Of course that is just a hypothetical conjecture. The term "soul" is being used only because nobody has come up with something better to call whatever it is that a human possesses that makes them, for lack of a better word, human. You can call it an essence, a spark, or thingamajig if that is your preference."

Okay, so never mind on the whole thing about how excited a theologist might be. I guess I spoke too soon; wouldn't be the first time.

"In any case, whatever that energy is that made you a living thing, you no longer have that inside you."

"Okay, I get it, but what does that have to do with why I can't be possessed?" I asked what felt like a perfectly logical question.

"It is that source that a demon or spirit infects and takes over. Sure, a demon or spirit could enter you, but it would have no anchor and simply be able to come along for the ride. It would have no ability to control you or force you to act against your will," Nancy explained. "The term possession is really not that accurate. The spirit does not so much assume absolute power over some poor human as it does infect their being and turn them into a twisted version of themselves."

That actually made perfect sense. It also explained why Chantal has been able to set up inside me sometimes when she feels that something exciting might happen that will transfer well into one of my stories. From inside me, she could watch things unfold and then write the accounts of what she witnesses (often much more clearly than I might've been able to convey to her in my own words).

"Ava!" a voice called with a bit of urgency. I recognized Queen Kari's silky tone right away despite that tinge of desperation that nipped at the edges.

"I wish I had more time to figure this out," I rasped, doing my best to force my vocal cord to obey and sound like me. Instead, I just sounded like I was in the middle of a puff-puff-pass line.

I hopped out of the van and saw a woman that made Eileen seem small by comparison. I doubt I had ever seen a woman that came close to seven feet tall...until now. This one had the long blonde braids dangling from each side of her head which was capped with a horned helmet. Her face was broad with a scar that ran from right about the left temple across the dented bridge of her nose and added a little extra width to the right corner of her mouth. Despite that awful blemish, she was still kind of pretty.

She wore a metal breastplate, and a fur tunic underneath that ended at the mid-thigh. She also had a few well-situated leather straps that appeared to hold everything in place. In her hands was a nasty looking battle-axe. One side had the huge curved blade and the other had that little spikey thing. The top of the axe's shaft was capped with a skull of something that I was pretty sure had to be some sort of lizard creature with nasty fangs.

"What is this?" the Valkyrie snarled, her eyes darting from Queen Kari to me with curiosity.

"This is Ava Birch, and she is my designated champion," Karidilean Qu'Shen, Queen of the Shamadiel Forest replied with a regality that squashed that previous tone of desperation.

"B-b-but—" one of the onlooking Valkyries began to protest.

"I am perfectly within my rights to declare a champion," Queen Kari snapped, cutting the Valkyrie off.

"So be it," the Nordic maiden, who was apparently going to be my opponent, finally agreed with a shrug. "My blade cares little about whom…or *what* it kills." She turned to me with disdain blazing in her eyes and set her mouth in a thin line that almost hid any trace of her lips. It also made her scar twist in such a way that only made her that much more visibly attractive; or maybe it was just the confidence that she seemed to have gushing from every pore.

Am I right on this, ladies? A hot guy can lose a few points fast if he lacks confidence (or thinks that being an egotistical asshole equates self-assurance) just as an ordinary guy can gain points on the hotness scale if he is intelligent and poised. We even like a bit of sensitivity if it doesn't go overboard and turn into him just being a great big sissy.

But back to this woman; she was hitting on all cylinders in the self-confidence part. I would need to find a way to use that against her. It was clear that she saw me as practically no threat.

There was a large area surrounded by the other Valkyries as well as a dozen or so elves. Standing by themselves were the two vampires. At least it was just the two of them at first. A large shadow emerged from around the corner of the abandoned building that shielded our little battleground. It was easy for me to see Eileen since my ghoulish vision is just as clear in darkness as yours would be outside on a sunny day. The Templar gave me a curt nod and then took her place beside Nancy with her hands clasped behind her back.

"We who are about to die salute you," I muttered.

Of course I had no plans of dying; but then who does? Not many people wake up in the morning and say, "Hmm…I think I'll kick the bucket today."

"Shall I make this quick, or do you prefer a slow death?" the Valkyrie asked as she swung her battle-axe back and forth like a giant pendulum. She started with it in her right hand cocked back over her shoulder and then let it swing downwards where she easily switched it to her left hand so that it could continue in its upward arc until it was cocked high in the air once again, then it would swing down and switch hands before stopping back where it all began. She did this with every three steps and I was wondering what on earth the purpose of that might be until she suddenly bounded for me and brought it up over her head and then down with a tremendous chop that would have split me in half if I hadn't danced back just as fast. She'd been basically hypnotizing me with her actions to catch me off guard!

Faster than any human, she reversed direction on her swing, brought the axe high and then took another swing crossways that would have lopped my head off if, once again, I'd not been just a little faster. In the instant where she had to try and slow her swing and bring it around once more, I slipped in and slashed across her middle with my right hand. My switchfingers raked the armor but did not cut into it at all. Even more discouraging, there weren't even any marks to show that I'd scored a hit.

I had to avoid another fierce swing of the axe; and this time I rolled forward and under her arms. With her back to me, I tried another swipe with my left hand this time. Her bare legs were no match for me and four perfect lines of red bloomed on her left calf.

That earned me a slight grunt, but nothing more as the Valkyrie spun on me. This time she made no attempt to attack. Instead, she was now re-appraising me. I saw a trace of what might be respect in her gaze, but I could have just been tooting my own horn.

"You might make a good Shield Sister," the Valkyrie said.

"Yeah...I'm good." I gauged our distance and matched her slight advance with a retreat as we circled each other. "See, you guys are here at the bidding of Claude the Psychic if my guess is correct. And when I am done here, I'll be going over to his house and putting an end to his claim on this territory. Now, what I can offer *you* is the chance to walk away from all of this and let me finish him off. Once he is dead, you won't have any need to come after little Queen Kari over there." I hiked a thumb towards the elf standing in the midst of her guards.

"That would be a dishonor to our names," the Valkyrie sniffed. "We are warriors who live by a code."

"Jeez, you are as bad as a man. Seriously, you aren't going to win this fight, and when I finish you, I'll end up eating your body. You really think that is a good deal."

"Better to die in battle than to be a coward and surrender." The Valkyrie arched an eyebrow at me and her lips curved in a slight smile. "And I have found that most people who start trying to bargain their way out of a fight when it has barely begun do so out of weakness and fear."

"Idiot," I breathed, lunging to the left to avoid her sudden swing.

I rolled and came up, my mind suddenly awash in rage. Great, Boudicca is trying to use my current distraction to free herself. Only, she was failing. That was a problem, because I could feel her anger turn to frustration. That same emotion coursed through me and made my attempt at leaping over the Valkyrie a bit of a fail.

I'd intended to land just a few steps beyond her so that I could try to get in another slice to the backs of her legs. If I could hamstring her, this fight would be all but over. Unfortunately, I landed in the midst of several of the other Valkyries.

Suddenly, it was a pro-wrestling lumberjack match. One of the women shoved me hard back into the open area where the fight was taking place. My opponent did not miss the chance to take advantage of the opportunity and brought her axe around once more. I heard it whistle past my ear and then felt something snap in my right shoulder.

I looked down and felt a surge of horror jolt me as I saw that the axe was actually embedded in my right shoulder. It hadn't gotten more than a few inches before bones brought it to a stop, but that was such a small consolation.

The pain was instant and made my vision blur and narrow. I heard a gasp from somewhere, but it was very possible that gasp was me…just before I screamed in pain.

Something in my head exploded in unison with that pain and I felt a tingle shoot through me like an electric current. The next sound from me was rage, and I stared into the eyes of the Valkyrie who was now smiling as she applied force and tried to bring me to my knees using the embedded battle-axe as a lever.

My brain was spinning as I tried to find my way to Ava Land. It was useless as the being within me continued to pour her rage into me despite the fact that I could sense that she was still secured where I'd locked her away.

I felt my left arm shoot forward. Two of my switchdigits snapped on the armor, but three found a way past the breastplate and plunged into flesh. The Valkyrie's expression changed in an instant, and I felt the warmth of her lifeblood as it poured over my hand. Before she could jerk away, my feet came up and all my toes dug into her bare thighs.

"You should have taken my offer," I said as Sharkmouth opened wide.

Before she could even gasp, I opened further and bit down, her entire head filling my mouth as I bit and then shook her like a great white might to a baby seal.

"Oh, my God," I moaned as the stump of her neck shot a geyser down my throat. For some reason, my brain equated it to a "whip hit" as the power of the Valkyrie's lifeblood sent its healing influence to the terrible wound.

I dropped to my knees and screamed in triumph as I jerked the axe free and let it drop to the ground with a loud clatter; much like a rapper might do with a mic after a particularly good line. In other words…the show was over. I hunched down and lopped off one arm, shoving it greedily into my mouth as I locked eyes with the remaining Valkyries. As I ate, my mind busily blasted the song *Sabotage* by the Beastie Boys. I really have no idea why, but for some reason, that is what kept me occupied while I ate.

As I wolfed down the second arm, I reflected on this whole situation. I wonder what a shrink would say to the fact that I eat to heal my pain. I'm pretty sure that's a thing.

"This is some sort of evil sorcery!" one of the Valkyries finally shoved her way through the group and stopped with her hands planted on her hips in what I always consider the *Wonder Woman* pose. She was glaring down at me with her teeth actually bared in a snarl.

I would have loved to respond, but I was taught that it isn't polite to talk with my mouth full. So, instead of saying anything, I went to work on one of the massive legs. The pain was almost gone by now, and I could feel the tingle of my bones knitting back together. Fortunately, I didn't have to say anything; Queen Kari stepped to my side. That sort of impressed me about the elf queen considering the fact that I was in the act of devouring a Valkyrie.

"Ava Birch acted as my champion, and at no time did she violate any of the rules. There were no spells cast. She is a ghoul and her body is her weapon." The queen actually placed a hand on my shoulder, but I pulled away, not really liking how that simple act almost made it seem like she was regarding me as some sort of pet. Seriously, if she would have patted my head, it would have been almost the same thing. Maybe I was just being touchy, or perhaps it was residue from the rage that was now all but gone.

I plopped down on my butt at that realization. Everything had been such a blur that I hadn't even realized that Boudicca's presence had dwindled and was once more totally confined to where I had her locked away in that box in my head. I also noticed that the black veins had faded. That was a fact I would definitely file away as important. I poked around a little deeper and was more than a little bummed to discover that I still could not sense Blodwen, Cody, Butt Pimple, or the others.

"...demand satisfaction! She has eaten Arifra which will now prevent her from returning to Valhalla and taking her seat at the table with the great warriors of our people," the Valkyrie was almost shouting. At some point, she had come to stand directly over me. It was time to put a stop to things.

I looked around and was surprised to discover that I'd obviously chowed down on the rest of my opponent. There was nothing left but the twisted remains of her armor. Hmm….that means that I'd gorged on her torso and then spewed up the Valkyrie's outfit without realizing it.

I hopped to my feet and stepped in between Queen Kari and the angry Valkyrie. She had more than a good foot on me in the height department, but I'd long learned that such things were really overrated when it came to a fight. Plus, I'd just taken down the biggest and presumably baddest bitch of the bunch.

"You *demand?*" I scoffed. "I am pretty sure I could still eat, so if you want to be next, you and I can throw down right now."

Throw down? Where did that come from? I wondered. Seriously, somebody my age should not be saying things like that. Sort of like when forty-year-old men wear baseball caps backward. Unless you are Ken Griffey Jr., you should really stop. It just makes you look like a douche.

"Ava," Queen Kari whispered, "the battle is over and you have won. Do not tempt fate by challenging another Valkyrie. They have very strong codes when it comes to fighting and challenges."

"Tempt fate?" I spun on the queen. "Maybe you weren't paying attention, but I handled things quite nicely."

"You almost ended up being cleaved in half," the elf queen reminded.

"Well…yeah…there was that part," I sort of stammered.

It's funny how fast we can put the unpleasant things behind us and move on to our victories. That is sort of why I get tired of hearing all those people on the daytime talk shows when they whine and cry about something from when they were six being the reason they are now drugged up losers who can't keep their legs together and end up having to use a paternity test that involves seven or eight guys to then find out that NONE of the them are the father.

"Listen up!" I shouted, making sure to do a complete scan of the crowd. "I know that you have been brought here by Claude to try and kill Queen Kari." I pointed to the elf as I climbed up on top of a rickety green Dumpster. "So here is my offer. Stop what you are doing for twenty-four hours. I am not saying to abandon your quest or whatever the hell you want to call it. I am simply asking for you to put things on pause for one day. By then, Claude will be dealt with, Queen Kari will be the new Psychic, and you can go back home to wherever it is that you came from, no harm, no foul."

The Valkyries gathered into a cluster with the exception of the one who had been doing all the complaining. I could hear everything they were saying, but I chose to try and tune them out and give them some privacy as they debated my offer. Besides, I'd heard enough in the first few seconds to know that they were almost unanimous in their decision to give me my request.

"To sweeten the pot, I have this." I reached inside my pocket and pulled out the bracelet. From the gasps, it was clear that the Valkyries knew exactly what I held. "Now, I could have been sneaky and clever and tried to put this on whoever seemed to be the leader of your group, but instead, I will give it to you as my promise that there will be no deception between us. I will deal with you honorably if you will agree to do the same."

At last, one of the Valkyries separated from the group and came to stand in front of my perch. She shot a pretty nasty look at the one who had skipped out on the debate and then returned her attention to me.

"We agree to your terms, but we have one of our own." The Valkyrie glanced back at her companions who were now acting strange. They were like nervous schoolgirls which, if you have never met a Valkyrie, you might not see what the big deal is, but trust me when I tell you that it just does not look right.

It sort of reminded me of Liam Neeson in *Love Actually*. If you have only seen him in those action flicks, then you might really be thrown off by his character in *Love Actually*. He plays this moping sort of a doofy dad who just lost his wife and finds therapy in helping his son woo his first crush. Of course there is also Andrew Lincoln. Could his Mark character be any more different than his Rick Grimes character from *The Walking Dead*?

"Okay, what are your terms?" I folded my arms across my chest and tried to sound like I was in charge of this whole scene.

"We have become fond of this peculiar game known as roller derby, and we wish to finish the season," the Valkyrie said, actually sounding nervous.

I considered their request and was trying to see a problem with it. Before I could answer, Eileen pushed her way through the Nordic women and wedged herself between me and them.

"You can skate, but no powers. That means you wear only human gear...no magic breastplates or helms that enhance your strength," the Templar stated.

"Wait…so their power comes from their armor?" I gasped.

"Of course. Without it they are basically mortal." Eileen turned to face me with an expression that read how she could not believe that I did not know this little nugget of information.

I did not know whether to be angry or amused. I decided to just play it off. "Sort of like your Templar ring," I quipped as I hopped down from the Dumpster.

That Ghoul Ava on a Roll!

12

Turn the Page

The car sped along the highway. Nancy, Tish, and I had not even bothered to say thank you or goodbye to the elves who drove us back to the vampires' house. We had until sunrise to finish this off. I needed to take Claude down and then hand over control to Queen Kari.

"Can I ask you a question?" Tish turned around in the car to face me.

I stopped staring out the window at all the passing scenery and met the vampire's gaze. Her eyes went wide with the slightest hint of surprise. I often forget that vampire's use their gaze to hypnotize their thralls. They are not used to anybody or anything looking them in the eye when they speak. Come to think of it, I did not recall Morgan ever looking Belinda in the eye when they spoke to each other. I would have to pay closer attention to that in the future.

"Sure." I didn't see any harm in answering questions.

"Why do you put yourself at risk the way you do?" Tish actually folded her hands across the back of her seat and rested her chin on her arms as she waited for me to answer.

"What do you mean?"

"Well, you came here on behalf of some human. You are also supposed to execute the current Psychic for the area and then hand over power to an elf. You fought a Valkyrie in solo combat and almost got chopped in half for your trouble. I've heard tales of the ancient ghouls. They were warlords and served no one. They bent others to their will and were served. You don't seem to have any desire for power, and given just what I know about ghouls, you could rule the world if you chose."

I considered her words. It was a reminder that I would definitely need to do some studying when I got home. I was horribly ignorant of what I was and lacked even the basic knowledge of my heritage, history, or whatever the heck you want to call it.

Plus, since I was not entirely sure what I was going to do about this latest development regarding the possibility that I might, for no reason I could come up with, have the grandmother of all ghouls living inside my head, I needed to get educated. I would need to read up not only on ghouls, but it would probably not hurt to find out what the human history books had to say about Boudicca.

"Why would I want to rule the world?" I finally replied. "I don't watch much television, but it seems that when I do, there is always somebody bitching about how politicians can't do their job. If you catch that much heat as a state senator, governor, or, God forbid, the president, how much crap would I have to listen to if I ruled the whole freaking world?"

Tish stared at me for a moment like she thought I might be joking. Her expression was a mix of confusion and disbelief. At last, she spoke again. "You would not be some ridiculous elected official. Your rule would be absolute and infallible."

"You mean like the pope?"

Now she squeezed her eyes shut. I was familiar with that expression. I'd certainly seen it enough when I was human. And if Morgan showed more emotion, I am pretty sure that look would be permanently etched into her face by now.

Frustration. Tish was meeting the self-proclaimed idiot child of the Supernatural world.

"Like the Caesars of Rome...your word would be law. There would be no democracy...no vote."

"Why would I want something like that?"

130

"How could you not!" Tish almost exploded.

"That's enough," Nancy scolded out of the side of her mouth like she could actually say something in this car and me not hear it.

"No, Nancy, it's okay," I spoke up. Then I returned my attention to Tish. "Maybe it is the whole thing about me being new to the Supernatural community, so perhaps I am still too rooted in my old human ways, but history has shown time and again that trying to take over the entire world is doomed to eventual failure. And maybe you have been away from your human roots too long to realize that the human race has come a long way in the past few decades."

"But they are sheep! Their minds are so easily swayed. All you need is a few fiery words and you will have devoted followers willing to die to further your cause," Tish countered.

"And those people are nuts!" I may not watch much television news, but I wasn't totally blind to what went on in the world. Did she think that I wanted to become some sort of Ava Bin Laden? "If I do anything, if I can accomplish anything, I would like to be able to see the people of the Supernatural world be able to come out of hiding. I think many of us have things to offer society."

"Just like the prophecy," Nancy whispered.

"Yeah, I don't know about any of that, but wouldn't it be nice if you could come out of the shadows?" I shrugged my shoulders and sat back.

Tish was apparently finished with the conversation as well because she turned back to face the front. I stared at the back of her head for a moment, but my mind began to sift through the possibilities of bringing the Supernatural world into the mainstream.

Who was I kidding? Our culture was entrenched in separation. For all we tried to claim in regards to being enlightened or tolerant, deep down, we thrived on division. We still fought over gay marriage and how many minorities got nominated for movie awards. What would trying to bring vampires, faeries, trolls, and goblins do to our already divided society?

I knew that I wasn't the first to consider the possibilities. If you have read enough of this sort of story, then you know how many Supernaturals hold on to the pipe dream of the world accepting us and not seeing us as monsters.

We continued along down the highway and a strange noise snapped me from my musings. It actually took me a while for me to realize that it was my phone. I reached into my pocket and pulled it out, staring and the words "UNKNOWN CALLER" on the screen.

I swiped it with a finger and answered. "Hello?"

"Ava?" a familiar voice exclaimed.

"Race?" Why on earth would he be calling me?

"I just heard from the local Templar commander in Dallas that you mixed it up with a Valkyrie." There was a hint of approval and, if I was hearing correctly, he even sounded a teensy bit impressed. But there was something else. I would swear that I could detect the slightest trace of fear in his voice. But even that wasn't it. There was something about him that simply sounded…wrong.

"That local Templar wouldn't be named Eileen would it?" I asked, still wondering exactly why Race Mitchell was calling me.

"She tells me that you and a goblin helped her deal with some revenants. Your little trip to Texas is turning into quite an ordeal. And now you are supposedly heading off to confront the local Psychic?"

"Why are you asking, seems to me you have all the information."

"Yes, well I just want you to know that there will be a detachment of Templars in the area. Since you probably were not informed, I felt it best to let you know that, should you win, they will make themselves known and ask you to agree to a standard information sharing pact that Templars often make with regional Psychics."

"You do know that I won't be staying here as a Psychic. I am only here to remove Claude and then hand it over to the elf queen that is a friend of Morgan's." There was an uncomfortable pause, and once again something nagged at the back of my mind that was trying to warn me.

"Would you consider staying on as the Dallas Psychic?" he finally asked. "A few of the Templars have met, and we believe that this might actually be a good move for you. This would give you a tie to our side of this little division and allow more of the Templars that are still on the fence to see you in a better light. Making that pact with us would be a huge PR move."

I couldn't believe what I was hearing. Why would Race want me to become a Psychic? Something was not adding up. When the realization struck, I almost laughed. I decided to hold off for a moment. I wanted to see what the end game of this call might be.

"You know very well that I can't abandon Morgan." I was really hoping that my caller took the bait. "She and I have been through a lot and built a strong sense of trust between us."

"And there is no reason that can't continue. Perhaps if you just stay on for a few weeks and see if this might be a good fit," the caller replied.

"How are you doing that, Hector?" I finally asked. "Honestly, your impression is spot on. You almost had me."

"What gave me away?" a voice that was definitely not Race Mitchell finally spoke.

"For one, you don't breathe. You have been a vampire for so long that you are simply used to the idea that you don't require taking air in your lungs. You would be surprised at how often a human takes a breath when they speak. It's really very subtle and something that you don't notice...unless they don't do it at all." That had been the one thing tickling my brain at the start of this call. I had not heard any breathing on that end of the line.

"It would seem that my reports on you are a bit misleading," the voice on the phone had become very silky. It was like audible sex. "So, perhaps I will put my actual offer on the table."

"Actual offer?" I doubted that there would be anything this guy might offer that I would be willing to accept, but it was always fun to listen to what people (or monsters) *thought* I wanted.

"If you are successful in eliminating Claude and assume control of this region, I have a Kiss of thirty that will swear allegiance to you if you abandon Morgan. Her time is coming to an end and I am giving you the chance to be on the right side of this conflict."

"What is the deal with Morgan? Why is there a sudden interest in taking her down?" It was time that I started getting some answers. Besides, if Morgan was in serious danger, and I could help put a stop to it, then maybe she would stop treating me like…hmm…

How did she treat me, exactly? Did I have a legitimate issue with her or was I simply letting old issues that weren't even a thing anymore cloud my judgment.

It was sort of like this thing that a girl named Stephanie Williams and I had when I was younger. For reasons that I don't remember, she pulled my hair when we were in third grade. I can't recall any of the particulars, but we ended up in different classrooms for our fourth, fifth, and sixth grade years. When we got to junior high, I hated her the moment that I saw her. It didn't matter that we were such different people by then, there was just that deep-seated hate from something silly that happened years before that threw up an instant wall between us.

Granted, my relationship with Morgan was a heck of a lot more complicated, and it was also still very new; but we had actually made progress. She didn't talk down to me nearly as often as she did (or that I *felt* she did) in those early days. Plus, she had even been nice to me a few times. Granted, I basically saved her life, but that only feeds my theory that our relationship is a bit more complicated than I can actually explain.

The one thing that I did know for sure was that Morgan was what I considered to be a "good guy" in this crazy, Supernatural world. I'd had other offers to abandon her, and now I was starting to see all of them as somehow connected to whoever it is that wants Morgan taken out. I don't really know why, but I feel a sense of loyalty to her. Plus, at least I knew what I was getting when it came to Morgan. That was something I could not say for all these other people.

"I think I'm gonna have to decline. For whatever reason, I am throwing my lot in with Morgan. And now I will make you an offer…get out of town. I don't know how you are here, whether it is under some guise that you are using to trick Claude or if you are an actual invader, but the moment I kill Claude, I have a feeling that I will be very aware of your presence and intentions. If you are not my ally, then you are my enemy and I will take you down."

Wow, I thought, *where is this new Ava coming from?*

I didn't have time to really give that a lick of serious thought. In the blink of an eye, Tish spun in her seat, her face a toothy sneer.

"Stupid bitch!" she hissed. In a flash, she produced a stake and drove it into Nancy's chest. I doubt the vampire even knew what was happening. That is what I will tell myself to feel a little better about her sudden and permanent death. Unfortunately, that left me speeding down the highway in a car that now lacked a driver.

For an instant, I was anticipating the vehicle slowing now that there was no foot on the gas pedal.

"Fucking cruise control," I managed as the car veered to the left and, just my luck, right in front of a big ass eighteen-wheeler.

That Ghoul Ava on a Roll!

13

You Spin Me 'Round

I felt the car start to slide sideways. The wheels on the driver's side took that moment to try and assert traction. That was what started us flipping. Over and over we went; it was like that time my babysitter convinced me that getting into the dryer and having it turned on was as fun as the rides at the amusement park. To add to my misery, Tish had taken the same stake that she'd just ended Nancy with and drove it into my chest. I guess she was hoping that I had the same weakness as vamps.

Nope.

I felt the Boudicca Box begin to thrum with energy. I decided to risk it and attempt to channel that energy into something useful. As the Go-Go's began to assert the fact that their lips were indeed sealed, I yanked the stake from my own chest with a howl of pain that I was unable to suppress.

Being a good girl, I'd put on my seatbelt. So, as the car finally stopped flipping over and came to rest upside down, I dangled in the back seat. Tish had not been obeying the traffic laws, and therefore, she was crumpled up and wedged between the roof which was now sort of a floor, and the front seats.

"You know, I never really liked you," I said as I reached out and grabbed a handful of hair. I pulled her up and drove her own stake into her chest. She sizzled and became sparkling dust in a matter of second. Her dying scream still lingered in my ears.

I used my fingers to free myself from my seatbelt, and quickly regretted that move as I dropped to the roof that was now the floor of the car in a heap. The hole in my chest was incredibly painful, and no manner of distraction could totally eliminate the sensation. I even switched to my beloved Brett and company as *Fallen Angel* echoed in my head.

CEASE THAT INFERNAL RACKET!

Crap, Boudicca was getting free. I was spread too thin. If I didn't feed, I worried that she might escape completely. I emerged from the wrecked car and took a look around. The wreck was worse than I thought. I counted five cars scattered about. A few good citizens had stopped both beyond and just before the scene. I would need to act fast.

I shot a glance at the car I'd been in and felt a pang of sadness for Nancy. I could deal with that later…right now, Ava hungry! I spied a car on its side about twenty feet away and literally leapt to it from where I was standing. I looked in and frowned. The kid behind the wheel could not be more than seventeen. He was clinging to life. His passenger was a girl of about the same age. She was dead, but I couldn't do it.

I bounded to the next car and my super sniffer was spot on. The man in the front seat had not been wearing his seatbelt and the steering column had crushed his chest. I took a quick look around and then dropped inside, ignoring the little cubes of shattered glass. I debated just eating him here, but worried that I would be discovered.

I pulled him free and hoisted him over my shoulder as Sebastian Bach wailed about the pains of *18 and Life* in my brain. That was not being received with anymore appreciation than the last song and I heard Boudicca howl her protest. Her cage was fading. I needed to eat soon.

I was in the scrub that grew along the side of this little stretch of road and took one final look around before settling in to eat. I could feel my body mending as I wolfed down the corpse. I didn't even bother to undress the poor guy and paid for it by having to regurgitate everything. In the midst of his clothes

I spied a wallet and scooped it up.

I knew I could absolutely do with another body, but already the strobing flash of red and blue lights told me that the first responders were on the scene. I sighed and bounded away as I restored the containment that held Boudicca at bay.

Now I had a new problem. I had to find Claude's house. I'd never actually seen where it was located. The first time that I came, I was inside a light-proof box; and when I'd left, I'd sort of transported out using a faerie corridor.

I was bounding along, staying parallel to the highway that Nancy had been driving down, but that was not going to do me any good. I was in mid-bound when I felt a slight tug inside my head. It wasn't Boudicca; that was all I knew for sure.

I stopped and tried to coax whoever it was inside my mind to come forward. As soon as I recognized the presence, I began to prepare guards if I had to seal this being away in a hurry.

There will be no need for that, Ava.

Mystify? How is it that you are okay and everybody else seems dead, or at least unable to communicate?

You had me sealed away. The primal ghoul was most likely not even aware of my existence, Mystify responded. He sounded old and tired. If not for what I knew about the former Psychic, I would have almost felt sorry for him.

I can get you to my house. Err...rather, I can get you to Claude's.

How do I know that I can trust you? I challenged.

You don't, but what reason would I have to come forward only to lead you someplace other than your destination? The voice went quiet for a moment before adding, *Besides, my fate is now tied to you. If you are eliminated, then I will cease to exist on any level. Funny thing about being faced with your mortality...you realize that there is almost nothing that you wouldn't do to extend it.*

I could accept that; at least for the time being.

In moments, I was loping along at something close to the speed of a cheetah with a sensation in my head that acted like a magnet and drew me to my chosen destination. Eventually I found myself on the edges of a very well-to-do neighborhood.

"Jeez, is everybody in this place a damn Cowboy fan?" I snorted as I sped past house after house sporting the gray and blue logo of the pro football team.

I passed flags, mailboxes, and one house with the insignia created on lights that took up almost the entirety of the roof. That same house had a very carefully manicured flower bed in the front yard. "That's just going a little too far," I scoffed as I loped past.

I slowed as Mysitfy's beacon indicated that I was now very near. I paused and looked around, taking in the view. Sure enough, the house at the end of a long driveway sat looking absolutely normal. The only thing that might have stood out as different would have been the number of and size of all the windows. It was almost as if the entire house was made of glass.

"Just Ava!" a voice hissed from some nearby bushes.

"Nose Wart! I hurried over and actually scooped the little goblin up in a hug. "I am so glad to see you!"

"Where are Nancy and Tish?" Devonna asked as she emerged from the same bushes.

"Yeah...about that..." I sighed. I took a deep breath and then told her what had happened.

"Then I am alone," Devonna almost wept as she uttered those words.

"On the bright side, that makes you the new Queen of the Kiss," I offered with as much cheer as I could muster.

"It doesn't work that way," Devonna sniffed. "The Kiss is created by those who are fit to lead. I am not a leader. That means I am to be claimed by whoever steps forward in this district." Devonna dropped her head and her shoulders actually began to shake.

"I will not allow you to be claimed by anybody if you do not wish it," Nose Wart stepped forward, his chest thrust out as he made this surprising declaration.

"I wish it were that simple." Devonna's head came up and I saw pinkish tracks running down her cheeks.

"We can sort this out later," I said. If I was being honest, I had no idea how I could possibly sort out something for the sad little vamp, but it was the only thing I could think of to say at the moment. "I need to know what you can tell me about the house. What have you seen since you've been here."

"I am ashamed to report that I have nothing," Nose Wart replied. "The house has been silent, and there has been no coming or going since we arrived."

"Then I guess I go in guns blazing so to speak," I muttered, not sounding at all confident.

I realize that I have been sort of a bad ass at times, but this was something else entirely. I had no idea how many and exactly what I would be facing. It doesn't matter how tough you are, there comes a point where you are simply outmatched.

"I will be at your side to the death," Nose Wart reminded.

"As will I," Devonna snuffled, her sad tone not inspiring any confidence at all.

"Then there is nothing left but to do it."

I started for the house, my ghoul hearing on full alert. Considering the fact that I was not hearing even the slightest peep from the house, I had to assume that there was some sort of magic involved.

When I reached the gate at the head of the driveway, I was debating on whether to jump it when an electric whir sounded and it swung inward. *So much for the element of surprise*, I mused inwardly as I started up the long, winding stretch of black asphalt with perfectly spaced and manicured trees along both sides that created a bit of a tunnel.

I heard it well before anything came into view; the padding of little feet coming at a sprint. Obviously Nose Wart and Devonna heard it as well. The vampire vanished with that amazing speed they possess. Nose Wart had his nasty little weapon in hand and edged just a bit closer to me.

"Come die, you infected anal sac lesions!" the goblin cursed, finalizing it with a massive, greenish loogie that he spat to the side of the driveway opposite of me. Good to know that, even in the throes of battle lust, he had the sense to aim that away from where I stood.

Sure enough, a small pack of goblins burst from around a corner of a very large six-car garage. They all had weapons drawn and were returning a variety of nasty little curses of their own as they charged.

I waited until the last moment and then leapt above the oncoming little monsters, coming down in their midst with my hands and feet slashing at everything that moved. I paid no heed to anything other than shredding every one of them. I only hoped that Nose Wart was smart enough to stay clear.

There was a blur on my left and I saw Devonna swoop in and snatch up two goblins—one in each hand—and then she was gone. Screams came from all around me as I ended at least a dozen goblin lives. Just as soon as it had begun, it was over and I was standing in a field of carnage. I saw arms, legs, heads, and torsos scattered everywhere. I was in the bull's-eye of all the fresh corpses and the smell was too much to resist as I plucked a body from the bunch and began to gorge.

Nose Wart was on the outside of the ring of death and after saluting me with his sword, he called out," May I join you in consuming the fallen, Just Ava?"

"Of course!" I managed around a head that burst in my mouth like a sweet, ripe grape as I bit down.

I continued to feast, but I realized that I was not feeling the familiar sensation of healing. I looked down and was amazed to discover that I'd not taken any injuries. If I had, they were so minor that I could not notice. Either that, or I'd actually gone through the entire skirmish unscathed.

I did not have time to think on that much as a window on the upper floor flew open and the sickly stink of vampire assaulted my nostrils. Only, these were not normal vamps.

"I am getting sick of revenants," I groaned as five of the creatures scurried down the outside of the house like giant, four-legged spiders. "I thought they were some sort nasty and embarrassing secret that the vampires were ashamed of or some such nonsense."

"In proper circles, that is the truth," Devonna appeared next to me, a trickle of blood that I doubted was hers ran from the left corner of her mouth and down her chin.

I waited for the pair that had obviously chosen me as their target and only briefly wished that I had one of my high-powered squirt guns full of holy water. I was suddenly very aware that I had not given enough thought to what I was walking into. After all, I knew that Claude had vampires. I'd seen the revenants that served him when I'd been his "guest" those many weeks ago.

The first one was the boldest of the pair and launched herself at me as soon as she was about thirty feet away. She landed a good five feet from me and that gave me time to lunge forward and slash with my left hand. I think we were both surprised when my blow took the thing's head off. It was still snapping its jaws when I plunged my switchfingers into its chest. That proved to be good enough and the horrible little vermin disintegrated.

The second revenant was apparently a bit smarter and took advantage of the death of his cohort. It had moved just a little ways behind me on my right side and then flew at me with teeth and claws. I felt something like scalding hot water on my neck and realized when the wet stickiness sluiced down my front that I'd been torn open. Being dead, my blood didn't really pump. Nor was it living blood. The revenant howled and flew back shaking its head and trying to spit out the foulness it had foolishly tried to ingest.

I took that moment to turn on my mental jukebox in order to distract my mind from the pain. Just as I plunged both hands into the back of the revenant and actually pulled out part of the spine along with a shriveled and useless heart, Paul Stanley was howling loud enough to drown out the sounds of battle as the song *Heaven's On Fire* exploded in my head.

I turned to see Nose Wart actually up on the shoulders of one revenant, his sword shoved into the mouth like a horse's bit as he whooped and steered it around in circles while the creature tried in vain to swat the tiny pest from its shoulders. Devonna had taken down the other two perhaps even faster than I, and was stalking towards the goblin. She was so intent on helping the little guy that she did not see the dozen or so large shaggy creatures coming up from behind.

Bugbears.

Basically they looked like gigantic versions of that cute little magwai from *Gremlins*...except for the two inch claws on each hand and the mouthful of razor sharp teeth. These were creatures that I could understand better than most when they spoke. They had deep growls, but they were surprisingly articulate; almost like Theodore the owlbear. The thought of that amazing creature had me wondering about his fate in all this madness. It had been clear that he'd sided with me when things had gone bad down in the dungeon of Claude the Psychic's home.

I had an idea on how I would deal with those big beasties. If it worked...yay me; if not, well, I better have a few songs queued up in my magic mental jukebox. I threw myself up and at the oncoming little horde, leaving Devonna and Nose Wart to hopefully finish off the revenants.

"Hi, boys," I purred as I landed about a dozen feet in front of the bugbears. They skidded to a halt, all of them bringing up a variety of long weapons that looked quite wicked. In fact, they reminded me of those things that the soldiers who served the Wicked Witch in *Wizard of Oz* carried.

"It is you!" one of the bugbears growled. Well, he could have just been talking; after all, it was a bugbear.

"Yes, and do you remember what happened last time I was here?" I wasn't sure that would help, but if I could at least stall them until Nose Wart and Devonna finished up with those revenants, then I'd have some help here in a moment or two. I doubted that I could take on a dozen bugbears on my own.

COWARD! I felt that box shifting and once more, Boudicca was attempting to free herself. I hated diverting any of my energy to keep her locked away, but I did not dare let her get free.

"You are alone, ghoul," the bugbear huffed and made a rumbling noise that I was sure was a chuckle.

"I was alone last time," I stated. Technically that was true, but that did not mean I didn't have a little help between the Templars, an owlbear, and a few other wee beasties.

"Ghoul or not, there is no way that you can face off with fourteen of us and have any hope of survival." The bugbear took a step forward. Something whizzed past my head and the entire skull of the towering creature seemed to explode.

"For the souls of Valhalla!" a female voice howled.

I spun to see a gang of breastplate wearing, helmeted women charging across the lawn. I had to duck as a hailstorm of flying hammers flew my direction and slammed into the wall of bugbears.

That Ghoul Ava on a Roll!

14

Bastard

I risked raising my head and taking a look. Not a single bugbear remained. Also, there were a few other creatures that, due to them not having much left from the neck up, it was impossible for me to figure out what they had been. No matter, they were dead now. Also, Nose Wart and Devonna had dispatched the last of the revenants.

"We have decided to make you a Sister of the Hammer," one of the Valkyries said as she stepped forward. I recognized her as the one who had done all the talking before I'd taken off to take care of this nasty business. I was now pretty sure that she was the lead Valkyrie...or whatever it is that they call their particular boss.

"I think we already discussed the fact that I won't be joining anybody nor doing anything other than completing this job and returning home to Portland," I said as I started for the house.

"You need not come anywhere with us, Sister Ava of the Handknives," the Valkyrie said affably as she fell in beside me.

Sister Ava of the Handknives; I liked the sound of that. Still, I was not ready to accept this honor that was now apparently being offered with no strings. Anytime you are given something with no supposed conditions, you can bet there will be a condition or two lurking underneath.

"I don't even know your name," I said as I gave Nose Wart and Devonna a nod of approval as they fell in beside me.

"I am Hildr, and I am the Shield and Hammer of Odin's Oski," the Valkyrie stated as she kept in step with me across the large, well-manicured yard.

"Umm, I hate to be the idiot sister, but what is an Ooo-ski?" I pulled up about twenty feet from a gigantic brick patio. The large, french double-doors were wide open. My brain quoted Admiral Akbar as it declared, *It's a trap!*

"The Oski is a wish fulfiller. We are the granters of the dying wishes offered by the warriors who are being slain in battle. It is our duty to choose those who distinguished themselves in battle and transport them to Valhalla," Hildr explained like it was a natural and normal thing.

"So...Valhalla is real?" I could not hide the little snort of amusement.

"Of course it is. There are many planes of existence that act as a waypoint for the dead. Many pass on to their own idea of an afterlife, some remain to pester the living, others are reborn in an effort to rectify misdeeds they are truly sorry for and some become warrior spirits who stand ready to combat the forces of evil and darkness that lie in wait to consume the world in that final day when Ragnarok is announced with the sound of Heimdall's trumpet."

I listened to all of what Hildr was saying as I scanned every window in search of any figures that may be moving about inside or waiting for us to enter so that they could spring whatever trap they had lying in wait. I simply decided that I was in no position to dismiss her claims or beliefs since I was already discovering that there was an entire world I'd always believed to be fiction that was far more real than any mortal human could possibly understand.

"Well, we can talk about this and Shield Sisterhood stuff when I have dealt with—" I was saying when there was a sudden and painful flash of light.

"Ava Birch," a familiar voice bellowed. "I am impressed. You have proven yourself to be everything that the stories and rumors are proclaiming."

I wanted to retort with something witty or maybe just plain sarcastic. Unfortunately, I was on my knees trying to bring up all my defenses as pain erupted throughout my entire being. I heard another wail of pain that I was only mostly sure did not come from me. However, I was in no position to make any sense of it at the moment.

For the first time, my mind was not skipping off to Ava Land. I was being consumed by the pain and it had gotten such a foothold that I was unable to force it away or isolate it.

"Nooooo!" another voice howled. I felt something collide with me. Whatever it was, it was trying to take me by the hands and pull me. Sadly, I could neither help nor resist, and so I felt myself move to what I could only assume to be my impending doom.

As sudden as the pain had come, it was gone and I found myself lying on my side in the dirt of a flower bed that ran along the front of that large patio that I'd just been approaching. It had a three-foot high wall that extended in a large arc that separated the yard from the brick area.

I looked up to see Nose Wart staring down at me with what I had to assume to be fear. That struck me as strange since goblins are notorious for not feeling fear. What could have possibly frightened my little sidekick?

"Wha…what happened?" I gasped as I tried to get to my feet.

"Claude has utilized one of the forbidden weapons," Nose Wart hissed. "He used a spotlight that is like the sun in its power."

"Ultra-violet," I murmured. I thought Morgan or Betty had told me a little about the rules in the Supernatural community. There were certain things that we were not allowed to do, and breaking those rules could result in serious consequences. Something told me that Claude didn't care about any of that.

"Devonna is gone," the goblin said as he helped me up. I was careful not to let my head pop over that wall…until I heard a massive crash.

"You are a dishonorable being, Psychic Claude Mortier!" Hildr exclaimed as another crash of what sounded like broken glass followed her last word. "If you do not wish to face the ghoul known as Ava Birch in single combat, then you are forfeit and our contract with you is now void, leaving us to enter this battle against you directly."

"As if you have not already, Hildr!" Claude's voice shot back. "Were those not your hammers that flew and took down my bugbears?"

"Those were merely minions. But now we can actually employ our weapons in an attack against your person."

That declaration was met with silence. I don't believe that Claude had thought this whole ordeal all the way through. There was a very long pause, and then the big light that had scorched me from head to toe went dark.

Nose Wart hopped up onto the brick barricade and walked along it with me as I headed for the little opening that would put me back on the giant patio. I kept my eyes fixed on Claude who stood peering down on me from a balcony on the second floor. Just to his left and being manned by what I was reasonably certain had to be a vampire was the ultra-violet searchlight.

"You must be Hector!" I called up, doing my best to mask my pain. It still felt as if flames were running across my skin in waves. I looked at my arms and expected them to be crispy, or at least blistered. They looked like they always did. That was odd.

The damage is internal, Mystify's voice came from what sounded like a million miles away. Behind his information, I could feel Boudicca. Actually, to be more specific, I could feel that she felt more securely confined and unobtrusive as compared to any time prior. I only had a second to relish that fact before a terrible shock to my body hit like a punch in the guy. And when I say "shock" that is exactly what I mean.

A blue crackle of energy rippled along my skin visibly and it felt like my hair was standing up and frizzier than a disco era home perm. The stink of ozone flooded my nostrils and I looked up to see Claude bring his hands together and start rolling something like he was making a very nasty snowball. And…he sorta was; except, instead of snow, it was balled lightning. The second such ball hurled at me, but this time all my attention was on Claude and so I easily ducked to the side and avoided being hit a second time.

With a great leap, I ended up on the rail of the balcony. That was perhaps not my best strategy. The vampire that had been manning the searchlight gave the big metal contraption a hard spin and clipped me just enough to knock me backwards. My arms instinctively pin-wheeled, but that didn't help much. A hard shove from the vamp finished the job and I toppled backwards and landed on the brick surface below with a painful thud that made my teeth clamp together hard enough to hurt and make me do a quick check of my mouth to ensure that nothing was broken.

I went to an old standby from my childhood. In a flash, the *Theme from SWAT* was blasting in my brain. Duh-nuh-nuh, duh-nuh-nuh, duh-nuh-nuh, duh-nuh-nuh…duh nuh nuh-nuh. I even heard the wakka-chikka guitar that was in almost every song that came out between 1974 and 1978. With that song cranked, I hopped up like a ninja from flat on my back to my feet in one of those cool moves you see in all the action movies, and then I dove into the house, smashing through the french double doors and sending glass everywhere. I looked around and realized that I had no idea where I was, but there were stairs going up to my right so I made for them.

I was just at the base of the stairs when that vampire from the balcony appeared. He flashed his fangs and appraised me with a look that bordered on disgust. Since I was basically used to that sort of reaction, it didn't really bother me that much.

"So, you survived Tish. That is actually quite impressive. If not for me, she would be the most powerful vampire in this district," the man called down to me as he began to descend the staircase.

"Yeah, you might want to get used to using past tense verbs when referring to Tish," I countered. "Then, with a smile, I added, "At least for as long as you don't fit into a Dirt Devil or a Dust Buster yourself."

"I will only make you this offer once, ghoul," the vampire that I now had to assume was Hector said with a fangy grin. (Yeah, making up adjectives is probably not my strong suit, but I gotta go with what fits.) "You can abandon this foolish errand. Perhaps Claude will find a place for you as he has for me. You might even discover life can be a great deal more enjoyable." He sort of waggled his eyebrows at me and I guess that was supposed to be suggestive. At least I think Hector believed that to be the case.

Unfortunately for him, all I could think of was Groucho Marx and his big, bushy eyebrows. That made me start to giggle.

"Yeah...not gonna happen," I managed between bursts of laughter that actually made my cheeks hurt.

"You have been warned." With that, the vampire used his crazy-fast speed and disappeared back up the stairs. I only had a moment to be puzzled.

"Ava, I am sorry," a vaguely familiar voice said in a whisper. A moment later, the lady who had called me down here in the first place appeared at the top of the stairs. She was straight out of the old B-movies in her long, flowing white dress that was so sheer it left nothing to the imagination.

"Brandy," I breathed, "what happened?"

"ENOUGH!" Hector's voice roared from someplace upstairs. "Kill her as I have commanded!"

Brandy started down the stairs. I could see the pink tracks of bloody tears carving their way down her face as I stood waiting for the attack. I really did not want to stake this woman. She was an innocent victim in all this madness.

"Is this what you wanted?" I asked as she walked jerkily down the stairs. It was obvious to me that she was actually trying to fight the command given to her by the vamp that I now had to presume was her maker.

"To kill you?" Brandy asked through clenched teeth.

"No." I shook my head. "I mean did you want to become a vampire?"

"Hell no!" the woman spat. "I have a husband and two children that I love. I have a life. This was my sister's scene. I hated it."

That was all that I needed to hear. I scanned the area and locked in on that open landing at the top of the staircase.

"Can you keep fighting this for a few minutes?" I whispered, not sure just how good vampire hearing might be.

"I'm doing all I can now," Brandy managed. "I don't know how much longer I have left. I feel more tired than if I'd been skating for a week straight."

I didn't say anything else. I grabbed the tall lamp in the corner and snapped it in half. I now had a very long, ugly, and somewhat unwieldy stake. With a single leap, I vaulted to the open walkway above. I shot a glance back over my shoulder and watched as Brandy slowly turned around and began her jerky march up the stairs. I would not have long before she was up here. I needed to act fast.

I took a sniff and locked in on the stench that could only be a vampire. I briefly remembered the fact that I would not be able to use that same tactic to hunt down Claude if he chose to run. I took a deep breath and upped the volume in my head as Simple Minds pleaded *Don't You Forget About Me*.

I had a sudden thought and acted on it. Taking a step back, I tensed my body and charged through the wall and into the room on the other side. Luckily, I had judged perfectly and not hit a single stud as the sheetrock exploded from the force of my collision.

"Hey, Kool-Aid!" I bellowed.

The male vampire was caught off guard. Maybe he'd known I was closing in, but he obviously did not expect me to come through the wall to get at him. I had a moment to take him in as I swatted the debris from my face and prepared to launch my attack.

He had jet black hair that was swept back into a ponytail. Admittedly, he did sort of have an Antonio Banderas thing going on in the looks department. He was in excellent shape and had his shirt open an extra button to show off his sickeningly perfect pecs. Too bad for him, all that did was give me a better target.

I lunged, bringing my stake in for the kill. It swished

through the air and missed completely as Hector recovered and danced easily out of the way. Yeah…I didn't think it was going to be that easy. I was about to try my best impersonation of a Venus Williams backhand when Hector was suddenly right in my face.

Crap, he had one of those ray gun thingies. He shoved the nose of it up under my chin. I did the only thing that I could think to do; I dropped to the floor like a discarded ragdoll.

The ball of energy melted into the ceiling with a harmless flash of light. I countered with a leg sweep and felt my foot hook his ankle. I gave it all I had and heard a surprising but satisfying crunch come as his leg gave way between the ankle and knee.

In my head, I heard Bullwinkle the Moose say, "Woo, sometimes I don't know my own strength."

I repeated my cool ninja move, and from flat on my back, I vaulted to my feet in a single, fluid movement. Hector was clutching his leg in obvious pain. I had to put my amazement aside at the fact that vampires could be injured. That just wasn't something that you saw in the movies. In one sudden lunge, I drove my stake down and into Hector's chest. He had barely enough time to look up at me and spit the word, "Bitch!"

Then he was a cloud of sparkly dust.

"Yeah…I've been told that," I mused to the pile of grit on the floor.

A scream from the doorway made me spin, ready to attack whatever was being thrown at me next. What I saw was Brandy on her knees. She was clutching herself tight with both arms and her head was thrown back as she wailed in obvious agony.

I took a step towards her when, just as suddenly as she'd begun, she stopped. Her body went rigid for just a second and then she collapsed to the floor in a heap. I waited for a moment or two just to make sure that she would not dissolve into dust. Nothing happened and I felt my body relax just a few degrees in relief. Hey, I wasn't sure how my killing Hector might affect the new baby vamp.

I could now leave Brandy and tend to my business. The windows were open wide revealing a balcony. I was pretty sure that it was the same one that Claude had been standing on earlier. I considered the stake on the floor, but decided against it. I was much more comfortable using my hands and feet than I was a weapon. Still, I scooped up the ray gun that Hector had tried to use against me just moments before. I had no idea if it would damage a Psychic, but there was only one way to find out.

I stepped out onto the balcony.

Sure enough, Claude was there waiting...sort of.

He was standing with his hands on the rail, his head down, and those long bleached blonde tresses hanging loose so that I couldn't see his face. He didn't even acknowledge my arrival.

"So...this is how the world ends. Not with a bang, but a whimper," he sighed.

"You're quoting Stephen King?" I asked with a sarcastic laugh.

His head popped up and he turned to me with a twisted look of scorn gouged into his face. "Stephen King? So you add further insult by being an absolute idiot!" he almost bellowed, but I did notice his eyes flick to the gun in my hand. "That is T. S. Eliot, you imbecile. What possible world exists where a hack like this King person can be credited to having written something penned by a genius?"

"Hey, I just remembered seeing the quote at the start of *The Stand*. Sue me."

"Perhaps it is best if I depart this world. If the fate of our community is tied to you, then I don't think that is a world that I want to live in," Claude spat.

"Hey, there is no reason for you to be nasty," I shot back. Although, come to think of it, I probably had bigger doubts than he did about the whole thing. The only difference is that it was *ME* thinking them.

It is one thing for a person to think something less than flattering about themselves, but quite another when somebody else voices it. For instance, guys, when we ask you if a certain article of clothing makes us look fat...the answer is ALWAYS no. Sure, we may go and change into something else anyway, but under no circumstance are *you* to express anything other than how wonderful and beautiful we look.

"Just do what you came here to do, Ava Birch, but before you kill me, let me just say that you are being used. You are nothing more than a pawn. There are two sides to this war, and you are only hearing what one side has to say."

"Maybe that is because the other side is trying to kill me," I shot back.

"And let me ask you this," Claude said as he stood tall and faced me, his lips pressed tight in stern disapproval as he took me in. "If you were on a ship and discovered that you could save everybody on board by offering your life...would you do it?"

"That question is stupid," I snorted. "It is so easy for people to say they would do it because the situation is so unlikely. The truth is, when it comes down to it, people are inherently selfish. Sure, there are the occasional heroes, but you only hear about them and make such a big deal because everybody else acted with self-preservation in mind. Very few people actually have what it takes to sacrifice themselves for the greater good."

"You will destroy us all, Ava Birch," Claude spoke the words like a judge passing sentence. It gave me a chill, or at least it creeped me out enough to make me momentarily consider ending him once and for all.

But did I really need to do that?

"I really am sorry for this," I said, and the funny thing is, I actually meant it.

I raised the gun and aimed it at his chest. He didn't even flinch. I briefly considered the words of that renegade that had been tied up in my basement. He'd said that this weapon only worked on the abominations such as the vampires and other undead. But Psychics lived unnaturally long lives.

So do the Templar, a voice said in my head from what seemed like a million miles away. *But the Templar has not died and then returned to life.*

Blodwen? I did not dare to hope.

What is left of me, the voice replied weakly.

I almost wanted to cry, but now was not the time. Right now I needed to finish dealing with Claude.

I dropped my arm that held the gun. In a way, I was very disappointed. Now I would have to kill him with my own two hands. Shooting him would have been so much easier. Using my claws changed everything.

Do it! Another voice howled from even farther away than Blodwen's. Great, Boudicca was back. *If you ever want a moment of peace, then you will kill this bastard and every other Psychic that holds a position of power. They are nothing more than slavers. They sit over their realms and use the Supernaturals under their control like pawns in a chess game.*

Actually, I had thought much the same thing. But then, does that mean I needed to kill Morgan?

Do not listen to that devil, Ava, Blodwen warned, her voice sounding strained and very weak. *Do what you came here to do and let's be away.*

I stepped toward Claude with my hands out wide sort of like I was coming to give him a hug. "You know, apparently you don't have to die for this to be over. I could find another way to beat you and claim the title. Hell, I'm not even going to keep it."

"What!" Claude barked. The only problem was that I didn't know what part of my statement had gotten his reaction. "You can't simply abandon your position. Once you assume the role of Psychic, you are magically bound to this region. If you leave it, after a period of time, it will start to drain you. Staying away for longer than a month is suicide."

Well, that was an interesting tidbit of information; I would have to keep that in mind. But that also told me what part of my statement had gotten a rise out of him.

"That is sweet of you to be concerned about my well-being, but actually, I will be passing my title on to another."

"So you were not here to kill the elf," Claude said to himself, his hands clenched into fists at his side. "Then I should have had you taken down as soon as you arrived."

"Why would I be here to kill the elf?" I asked, more than just a little curious.

"Ghouls and elves have never been friends," the Psychic laughed mirthlessly. "I knew that you would come to claim your position here sooner or later and just figured that you would rather square off against me than against an elf…and a queen no less."

"You just keep on showing how little you know about me," I replied. "You obviously based your assumptions on what you might have known in regards to ghouls of the past."

"The past!" Claude scoffed. "Are you so foolish as to think that you are the only ghoul in existence?"

I almost confirmed his suspicion by blurting out something like, "You mean there are others?" Instead, I crossed the room and reached out, grabbing him by the throat and pinning him to the wall. Whether it was actually me or I was being driven by one of my inner denizens, I am not entirely sure, but I wanted to end this conversation before he confused me more than I was already.

"Believe it or not, I never wanted this," I whispered as I stared into Claude's eyes.

Before he could say another word, I made a quick slash with one hand and removed his head. I started to relax and was instantly flooded by a wave of pain. I'd almost forgotten about the damage I'd received from that cursed spotlight. So, I did what ghouls do; I ate Claude.

15

Two Out of Three Ain't Bad

"You mean I am going to be like this forever?" Brandy wept.

"Basically," I answered as I sat down on one massive sofa. "The alternative is that I can end you, but I doubt you want that."

The woman actually seemed to consider my offer for a few seconds! I was trying to feel sorry for her, but I was too tired.

"I have opened the dungeons, Just Ava," Nose Wart reported, stopping in front of me with a welcome and familiar creature on his heels.

"Theodore," I greeted the owlbear, doing my best to sound enthusiastic. Fatigue was not something that I was accustomed to feeling, and it was making me less than cheerful despite my victory.

"I knew you would return to us," the furry and feathered creature huffed as he bent down to scoop me into his massive arm/wings.

"Okay, put me down," I managed to squeak. While I might not require air in my lungs for breathing, I still needed it in order to speak and the massive beast had squeezed almost all of it from me when he'd scooped me into an owlbear hug. (See what I did there?)

There were a few other assorted creatures roaming about.

Most of them had a dazed look of utter confusion on their faces. Many seemed lost and a few even looked afraid.

You need to declare your assumption of power over the district, Mystify's voice prompted. He walked me through the simple ceremony.

"I am Ava Birch and I proclaim myself the Psychic of this territory. All Supernaturals within my realm must enter only at my pleasure or face the penalty which can include death at my discretion."

As soon as the words were spoken, I was flooded with an overwhelming sensation that was at the same time singular points and an entire mesh of feelings, tastes, smells, and even a peculiar itch in the back of my head. I noticed all the Supernatural beings in eyesight turn to face me at once and bow like I was some sort of Mecca.

Actually, not all of the Supernaturals bowed. Nose Wart remained standing, as did Brandy. Funny, but the normal stench that I picked up from vampires had not only gotten stronger in my nose, but I could taste it in the back of my throat; and I did not like it one little bit.

She is an independent, Mystify explained. *Since she has no Kiss and serves no master, she is currently not under your jurisdiction.*

"So, Brandy, what will it be? Do you want to continue, or do I end you?" I asked.

"I don't want to die. But what about my family?" the woman asked through fresh tears.

I was at a loss, but once again, Mystify came to the rescue. I listened to his explanation and then related it to the poor woman.

"Yeah, you can't see them anymore. Not unless you plan to turn them, but it is highly discouraged…especially in the case of the children. Apparently child vampires can become quite a problem." Mystify hadn't elaborated, and I honestly didn't care. "Since you would have to reveal your nature, it is forbidden by Supernatural law. Only thralls can be allowed to live once your nature is revealed."

I wasn't surprised when this was greeted with more tears.

"Take your time and think it over," I said, doing a terrible job of sounding sympathetic.

I headed away, making the rounds among the assorted creatures and trying to distance myself from the stink of vampire. Nose Wart stayed at my side as I greeted the variety of creatures that included goblins, bugbears, and two adult fiery jötunns. I was glad those two hadn't been thrown at me. I was also a little curious as to why.

They are stuck inside the keep, Mystify explained. *Seriously, do you see any doors big enough for them to use as an exit. The only way out for them would be for them to bash their way out.*

So? I shot back. *Better to pay for home repair than end up dead.*

Oh, Claude never once believed that you stood a chance.

Yeah, well I hope folks keep on underestimating me.

After this little adventure, I doubt that will continue to be the case for much longer, another voice added weakly.

Blodwen, you're sounding better. I was relieved to hear her voice sounding less strained. I had yet to hear from Cody or Butt Pimple, and honestly, if I never heard from Adrianna again, I would be totally fine with that. Then there was Claude...would he be chiming in soon.

Charming...to the last, a snarky whisper drifted from deep within the darker corners of my mind. Well, there was The Queen of the Zombies. Time to box her back up.

I thought that you guys couldn't read my thoughts, I shot back with a bit of surprise.

You broadcast that very clearly, Cody offered. *Glad you actually care enough to worry about my well-being.*

Yes, well... I sort of let my thoughts drift. I had yet to hear from Butt Pimple and that had me concerned, especially considering the reaction Nose Wart had displayed when he'd peered into my eyes and seen his former mate.

"Nose Wart?" I stopped and turned to my little goblin friend. "Look into my eyes, please."

He turned to me, but I saw reluctance very clear in his expression. He actually sighed and slowly raised his gaze. For a

161

brief moment, he was sort of like a kid peering in a toy store display window. Yeah, I'm not sure if they even do those anymore, but that is the best I have right now.

"Well?" I finally asked, unable to read his expression.

"I do not see her, Just Ava," the goblin said, dropping his gaze to the floor.

Anybody got a bead on her? I broadcast inside my head.

There was a long and painful silence. At last, I heard a low chuckle that gave me a shiver. *The goblin bitch belongs to me now. If you want her...come get her.*

Crap, I thought, making a point to keep that little expletive to myself. I was not going to show weakness to Boudicca. Unfortunately, there was nothing that I could do about her right now. I knew that a Mind Walk was off the table at the moment. But I also knew that was a temporary situation.

Trust me, Boudicca, I will be there soon enough. And when that day comes, you are going to regret it.

I had no idea where the bluster and boldness was coming from, but I actually felt a little bit like a bad ass again, at least for the moment. The past several hours had been one heck of a ride, and I was still standing. And for the most part, I'd done this on my own.

"I am glad to see you have survived this ordeal, Ava Birch," a voice jolted me to the present.

"Queen Kari," I said, not bothering to turn around and face the elf. There was still a little something in my head from what Claude had said about elves and ghouls not being friends. I needed to wipe that thought from my mind for now and put on my "Happy Ava Face" and be done with what I'd come here for. "So, I see you aren't wasting any time claiming your territory." I turned around. Only, I think there was still a hint of that seed planted by Claude coming through in my voice because Queen Kari took a step back and actually looked afraid for a moment before she composed herself and plastered that regal expression back on.

"You are being well paid for your services," the elf spoke slowly, and it was clear that she was struggling to sound like she was in charge of things.

"And I will hand this territory over to you just as I said I would do," I replied coolly.

It was strange, but I was getting a vibe from Queen Kari that was a bit unpleasant and even a little uncomfortable. Between her and Brandy, it was like a migraine starting to build.

Neither has been officially invited into your territory, Mystify's voice called. *Both have come before you without your permission and so you are not yet able to reconcile their presence. You must either formally grant them permission to remain...or dispatch them.*

I'm pretty sure that I heard a thread of hope in the former Psychic's tone. I wasn't sure if it was for Brandy, Queen Kari, or both, and I was still just too tired to care. I fought the urge to lock him away since it was clear that he had good information, but that did not mean I trusted him a whit.

"Let me start by welcoming you to my region, Queen Kari, and you, Brandy McKeon," I announced. It was like a switch was thrown and the entire room went silent. I only had a moment to wonder if I'd done something wrong until Blodwen piped up.

You are fine, but as the Psychic, you are the closest thing to a king, president, or evil overlord that these individuals know. Your word is law and you have all the power.

I thought that a bit strange since I never got that vibe from Morgan, but once again, it was Blodwen to the rescue. *She has never claimed you, and from what I have seen, she keeps you away from the internal issues of her leadership. She only deals with you when she has a job for you to do.*

I banked that bit of information and turned to Queen Kari. "I will hand this place over to you as soon as I square things with the Valkyries."

I saw her face tighten just a bit around the eyes. It was clear that she was not a fan of this arrangement.

"You cannot simply hand this place over as you so quaintly put it," Queen Kari sniffed.

"Are you really gonna cop an attitude with me before I give you your new kingdom?" I shot back, taking a step closer to her so that I was well within her personal space. I even made it a point to ignore the elven archers who were now nervously fingering the bows they carried on their backs.

"And why can you not just do this now so that we can be done with it?" Queen Kari sniffed, sounding like a petulant child instead of any sort of royalty.

"I have something to tend to, and right now, I say who is welcome and who is not in this region."

***

I ducked under the elbow that came for my midsection and gave a hard shove using my shoulder as I careened into the powerful woman. I saw the two in front of me, but just as I was trying to figure out how I could slip past, Claire Lee Insane was whipped by me with a little help from Shirley Temper.

For such a little gal, Claire was almost like the human equivalent of a cannon ball and she sent both Valkyries in opposite directions. One of them hit the wall and flipped over it to the delight of the spectators. The other actually went flying into her bench that was situated in the big oval on the inside of the track. The Valkyries not on the floor all scattered instead of trying to catch her and the woman ended up tripping over the bench and face planting in what amounted to a painful looking belly flop.

I popped up from my crouch and brought my hands to my hips in a signal that the jam was over. Another chorus of cheers and boos echoed in the warehouse-turned-roller dome. I slowed and felt a hand come down hard on my back with enough force to almost knock me off my feet.

"Nicely done!" Eileen rumbled as she skated past. She tried to wink, but her left eye was already practically swollen shut from an earlier jam where she had gotten into a bit of a scuffle with the other pivot skating for The Valkyries.

"The final score...The Valkyries...fourteen...your Rumbling Renegades...twenty!" an announcer's voice boomed from the PA system.

Again, the crowd went wild with a mix of cheers and catcalls. I saw the trucker hat yay-hoos expressing their displeasure as they threw up their hands in apparent disgust. I winked at them as I rolled past with Eileen and Claire. We pulled up in front of Brandy who stood in the shadows of the concession carts. She came forward and flashed a smile. I returned it, but I still had to force back my disgust. For some reason, her smell continued to be just a bit stronger than what I was used to. I didn't know why, but it was really tough for me to be around the woman for very long.

"You're a natural," she exclaimed. "Are you sure that you don't want to stay for the season?"

"Naw, I need to get home, I have things there that need dealing with."

"I really wish you would reconsider," Eileen said with an uncharacteristically sad tone in her voice. "Maybe being here and holding this region isn't such a bad idea."

"That's not my thing," I said, but I must admit, there was a certain allure to it. "Besides, I have a few internal issues that I want to get a handle on and I know somebody back home that can help me."

"You do know that you could bring whoever it is out here," Eileen countered.

"Yeah, but I love the Northwest, that's really the biggest part of my decision."

I heard a cough behind me and forced myself not to react. Eileen wasn't so subtle and I saw her frown. After a few seconds, she looked back down at me and took my hand. "If you ever need help...don't hesitate to give me a call." With that, she and Claire skated away.

Brandy started to follow and then paused. "Thanks for all you've done, Ava."

"You're welcome, Brandy, and I am really sorry about..." I gestured to her with both hands.

"Not your fault, Ava."

"And I mean what I say about you being able to come back to Portland with me. I am certain that Belinda would take you into her Kiss. It really might be easier than being in the area and being tempted to drop in on your family."

"We'll see." And with that, she walked away to join her former team mates as they celebrated their win.

I turned to face Queen Kari and was just about to address her when another voice called out, "Ghoul!"

Now, she could have just been shouting the name on the back of my jersey, but since it was one of the Valkyries, I knew better. I turned as the woman rolled up to me. Like Eileen, she was gonna have one very nasty black eye before the night was over.

"Come to wish me farewell, Hildr?" I asked sweetly. Hildr had been the Valkyrie that I'd made the deal with after my little death match.

"No, I have come to ask you one final time to join us as a Sister of the Shield," the woman replied as she stopped in front of me. I had to suppress a snicker as she actually shoved through a trio of elves that were part of Queen Kari's bodyguard contingent.

"It really is a generous offer," I said with a shake of the head. "But I think I will just go back to being That Ghoul Ava."

"Well, then I want to give you this." Hildr reached inside her shirt and plucked a small baggie from someplace that I'd rather not think of; it was the bracelet made from Freyja's hair! "Wear it, and if ever you need us, simply call me by name."

"What, you're the only Hildr out there?" I scoffed, suddenly a bit nervous about accepting such a powerful gift.

"I am the only Hildr handing you this bracelet with a vow," the woman replied. She held out the baggie and I took it reluctantly. "Fight with integrity, Ava Birch."

I watched the woman skate away, uncertain as to how I had merited such an honor. I was so blown away that I guess poor Queen Kari ended up clearing her throat a few times before she actually got my attention.

"Huh?" I started. "Oh, yeah. So...how do we do this?"

"You must set the terms and then I must defeat you based on those terms if I accept," Kari replied, her voice now starting to regain some of its confidence and regality.

I was thinking it over when Nose Wart came strolling up. He had a huge grin on his face that made me wonder what he'd been up to. I didn't have long to wait as he reached in a pouch at his side and produced a very shiny gold coin.

"And where did you get that?" I asked as I got a glimpse of several such coins in the pouch hanging from his belt.

"From her guards." Nose Wart hiked a thumb over his shoulder at Queen Kari, and then turned to face her. "You might want to find some younglings that are not such cowards."

"I beg your pardon?" she stammered, obviously caught off balance by being told what to do by a mere goblin.

"None of them were willing to take the automatic win in Mumbly Peg," the goblin snorted.

"Umm…what?" I cocked my head in confusion.

Nose Wart displayed his left foot and I actually staggered back. It was a bloody mess. "Yeah…can't get any closer to your foot than to stick it. Nary a one of those pointy-eared sacks of bugbear scrotum pus had the nards to stick the knife in his own foot to claim the win." Nose Wart held up his nasty blade that was still glistening with relatively fresh blood.

I shrugged. What could you do? But that did give me an idea. It must have shown on my face because Queen Kari took a step back. "You' can't be serious!" she squealed.

I snatched Nose Wart's coin from his hand and looked at her with confusion before I shook it off and blurted, "Heads or tails."

The elf paused and then visibly relaxed. "Heads," she finally answered meekly.

I tossed the coin, caught it and slapped it down on my forearm. Removing my hand for us to see, I frowned.

"All right…best two out of three."

Two hours later, I rasped, "Okay…best one hundred and twenty-seven out of two hundred and fifty-three." I tossed the coin and let it bounce on the floor.

"Tails," Queen Kari groaned.

The coin landed, spun, and came to rest.

"Thank God," I exhaled. "Nose Wart, c'mon…we're going

home."

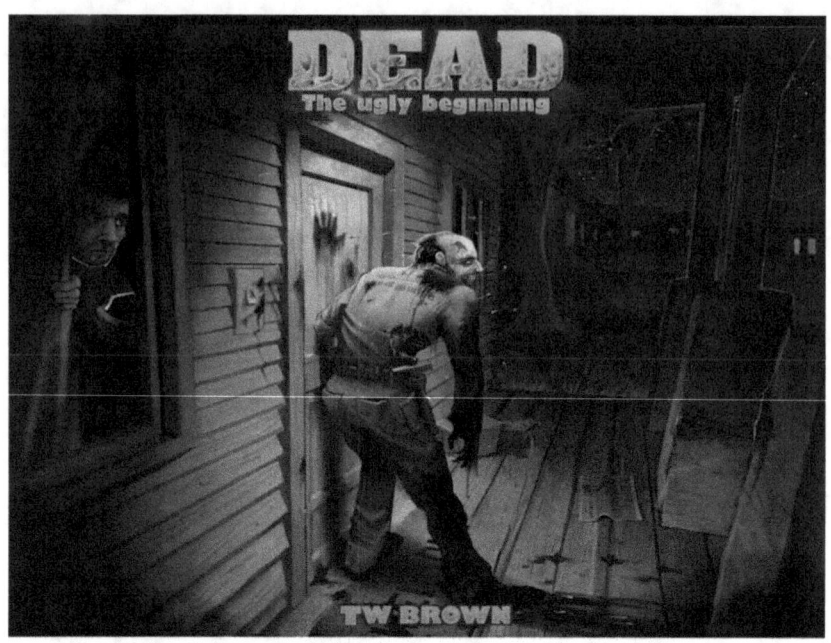

MAY DECEMBER

Publications

**The growing voice in horror
and speculative fiction.**

Find us at www.maydecemberpublications.com
Or
Email us at contact@maydecemberpublications.com

TW Brown is the author of the *Zomblog* series, his horror comedy romp, ***That Ghoul Ava***, and, of course, the ***DEAD*** series. Safely tucked away in the beautiful Pacific Northwest, he moves away from his desk only at the urging of his Border Collie, Aoife. (Pronounced Eye-fa)

He plays a little guitar on the side...just for fun...and makes up any excuse to either go trail hiking or strolling along his favorite place...Cannon Beach. He answers all his emails sent to twbrown.maydecpub (@gmail.com and tries to thank everybody personally when they take the time to leave a review of one of his works.

His blog can be found at:http://twbrown.blogspot.com

The best way to find everything he has out is to start at his Author Page:

You can follow him on twitter @maydecpub and on Facebook under Todd Brown, Author TW Brown, and also under May December Publications.